Praise for *Nothin...*

'A beautifully judged balancing act between revelation and frustration, making the reader complicit and terrified by turns . . . This one will stay with you like your shadow, as hard to shake off and as impossible to pin down'
Guardian

'I greatly admired Conor O'Callaghan's
Nothing on Earth, as fine as it is frightening'
John Banville

'Strange, beautiful and quietly terrifying . . .
I could not put it down'
Donal Ryan, author of *The Spinning Heart*

'An original story, brilliantly told . . . extraordinary, low-key and pitch-perfect . . . This adroit, uncompromising novel leaves questions unanswered and won't easily release its hold'
Irish Times

www.penguin.co.uk

Nothing on Earth

Conor O'Callaghan

BLACK SWAN IRELAND

TRANSWORLD IRELAND PUBLISHERS
28 Lower Leeson Street, Dublin 2, Ireland
www.transworldireland.ie

Transworld Ireland is part of the Penguin Random House group of companies
whose addresses can be found at global.penguinrandomhouse.com

Penguin
Random House
UK

First published in the UK and Ireland in 2016 by Doubleday Ireland
an imprint of Transworld Ireland Publishers
Black Swan Ireland edition published 2017

A CIP catalogue record for this book
is available from the British Library.

ISBN
9781784161460

Typeset in 11/14.5 pt Electra by Falcon Oast Graphic Art Ltd.
Printed and bound by Clays Ltd, Bungay, Suffolk.

Penguin Random House is committed to a sustainable
future for our business, our readers and our planet. This book
is made from Forest Stewardship Council® certified paper.

MIX
Paper from
responsible sources
FSC
www.fsc.org   FSC® C018179

1 3 5 7 9 10 8 6 4 2

If any man lie with a woman in her flowers, and uncover her nakedness, and she open the fountain of her blood, both shall be destroyed out of the midst of their people.

Leviticus 20:18

1

IT WAS AROUND about then that the door started banging. The wood shook with the banging. So did the letterbox's brass-plated inward flap. Even the cutlery in its open drawer, the delft drying on its drainer, seemed to tremble a fraction. It was a time when nobody called. Early evening, the hottest August in living memory.

On the other side, on a doorstep in the middle of nowhere, stood a story everybody already knew. And the form that story took, as they say, on the evening in question? Breathless skin-and-bone, a girl of twelve or thereabouts. Her tummy, her breastbone, the edges of her ribs, were all visible. She looked like one who had neither eaten proper food nor inhaled fresh air for years. Her teeth were yellow, her nails uncut and filthy. Her skin was sunburned, except for those white lines that had been covered by straps. It was also marked in places, her skin was: scratches, creases, streaks of dirt, and words.

There were actual words scrawled around her skin, dozens in blue, frayed at the edges, blurred by sweat and largely illegible. The more blurred ones resembled bruises. The more intact were like little darns meant to mend those points where the fabric of her flesh had worn threadbare. The words were not confined to her hands and wrists either. They were scattered all over her, and they were hard not to stare at.

'Come in.'

She was wearing fluffy panda slippers, a pair of light grey tracksuit bottoms smeared with black dust and food stains, and a man's bomber jacket that was easily five sizes too baggy. She was wearing, also, an odd shade of lipstick: a red-brown that hadn't been applied with any great care and served only to accentuate her air of wildness. Her hair was wavy jet black and quite long, halfway down her spine. But it had not, by the look of it, been washed for several weeks. Nor was her face particularly clean. Her eyes had black around them: liner, sure, but a lack of sleep as well. Their irises were a bottle green. Like emerald. The jacket hung down around her elbows, her whole torso exposed. A coloured silk scarf was knotted as a bikini around barely pronounced breasts.

And, of course, there were those words. The words had to have been in her own hand: they were in a childish print and they were upside-down, as if she had scribbled them on herself from above and given no thought to how they might look. It was impossible not to be a little scared of her. Which is crazy to say, considering that she was such a slip of a thing, and so obviously terrified herself. Terrified of what? Of me, I suppose, the man she had probably never set eyes on in her strange life before then, standing in front of her, inviting her to enter a nondescript dormer bungalow on a secondary road. Of the whole world, really. She noticed me trying to read the upside-down words in blue pen on her white skin and pulled the two sides of her jacket tight against her.

'Come in,' I said again, stepping backwards, holding my door open for her and gesturing with the other hand towards an invisible path past me that she, hesitantly, inched into. 'Do.'

She had run very fast to my doorstep: she was panting heavily, and her skin was glistening with perspiration. When she passed me, I caught the sharp whiff of baked syrup, stale urine and pure, naked fear.

I won't ever forget how that girl spoke. I still hear every word she uttered, precious few at first, in the weird intonation she had. She parked herself in an armchair in my front room, the one I usually sat in. She was perched on the edge of it, like a sick bird, and she was squeezing her jacket even tighter around herself.

'What's your name?'

'Helen,' she said. 'What they say.'

'What they call you?'

'It is my *mutti*'s name.'

Her English had a sort of freeze-dried quality. It was as if her every phrase had only just been taken out of the vacuum packing it had lain in for years, and was found to be almost too well preserved. It felt parched and brittle, lacking any binding moisture. Every now and then she would pause, appear to redden and almost wait for approval or forgiveness before finishing. And yet there was still an occasional lilt that, I would come to realize, she must have gleaned from listening to her mother and her mother's sister.

I went back into the kitchen, to get her a glass of something fizzy from the fridge. There was a tin of sweets lying on the table. I paused there, in my kitchen, and inhaled deeply to compose myself. I was just back, after performing the Saturday teatime slot. But on top of that was the shock of her hammering on my door, of the sight of her there on the step and the state she was in.

'Now,' I said, keeping my voice steady, returning to the

front room with a glass of orange mineral and the tin of sweets. She was staring at the swirls in my carpet. 'What's all this drama?'

'My papa is gone too.' She tried very hard not to start crying when she said this. 'One minute he is behind you. And next time he was gone.'

'What do you mean, *gone*?'

'Just gone. I looked all over the house.'

'Did you try calling him?'

'We have no more credit.'

It struck me, at the time, as one of several peculiar phrases she used. She said it as if credit were something held and frittered collectively, all at once. I couldn't altogether get away from the phrase's implication of belief or the lack of it. *We have no more credit . . .* Then there was that 'too' she had tagged onto her father's disappearance. Somewhere, buried deep in that 'too', was a cluster of implicit acknowledgements: that this wasn't a first; that she knew I knew that; and that she was aware of my and the whole town's fascination with her family.

'I'm sure everything will be fine,' I told her. Even to myself, my words of comfort sounded trite, hollow as anything. 'You did exactly the right thing, Helen.' I remember how oddly puzzled she looked when I used that name. So I did it again, just to test her surface. 'Settle yourself there, Helen, and I'll make a couple of calls.'

The local garda station was on answerphone. It was always. The message gave the number for the station in the nearest big town which would have officers on duty. The number rang a dozen times before anyone answered. But answer someone did, eventually, and I spoke to them.

There have been some who have tried to imply that I never made any such call, that the girl would be with me yet were it not for the intervention of the authorities. It was me who called them, within twenty minutes of the girl banging furiously on my door, and my call was logged in their duty register.

The officer on duty sounded barely out of his nappies. He made no bones, initially, of letting me know that he thought I was as daft as a brush. 'I'm afraid you'll have to run that one by me again,' he kept saying, and I had to work hard to maintain my manners. I told him everything, standing in the hall, even pulling the door of the front room shut and lowering my voice so that I could explain fully without the girl overhearing. He fairly jumped to life once the connection registered.

'Now,' I said, more than a little put out by his attitude, 'pass me on to somebody senior, like a good chap. You run off and process parking tickets.'

I could hear in the background a radio's litany of football results from across the water. An older voice, one I didn't recognize, came on the line. He said he remembered the particulars.

'So himself is gone now,' he said.

'So she says.'

'Since when is this?'

'Since twenty minutes ago,' I said. 'Just came banging on my door, in a right state.'

'Okay.' I could hear his ballpoint clicking. 'Sit tight,' he said. This one seemed to grasp immediately the seriousness of what I was reporting. 'I'll have someone with you in the next half-hour.'

My cleaner was already out and about, collecting her three sons from football, when she answered. She sounded staggered it was me calling. I never called. She and her sons were with us within minutes. They all came in, the boys with sticky jerseys, flushed faces and orange ice pops, staring at the girl in the armchair. My cleaner addressed a handful of well-meaning questions to her, but got the barest of responses. The girl just sat there, her face blazing with embarrassment and anger, staring intently at the telly that I had switched on for her distraction.

One of the lads asked, 'Where's your dad?'

'I don't know,' the girl said. In fact, I would say she growled it.

My cleaner made a face and I edged slightly towards the door. Though she was staring at the screen, there was the suspicion that the girl was still watching everything in the margins of her vision. We shepherded the lads back outside, where they climbed silently into a people-carrier.

'The authorities are on their way,' I whispered to my cleaner on the front step. 'I'll be sure to buzz you if there are any developments.'

I remember how bright it was standing out there, and how hot, with the sun just starting to set. There was also a lot of traffic at the supermarket across the road, voices and music through lowered windows, people getting stuff for their Saturday tea and tickets for the weekend lottery draw.

'I'll pop back later,' she said. My cleaner, that is. She has asked me not to use her own name, or any name for that matter. 'Not to leave you marooned with Madam.' She was always thoughtful that way. 'Himself should be back by then, and will be able to watch over these lads.'

The girl was still staring hard at the telly. I didn't pay much attention to what was showing. Some early-evening film suitable for families. Some comedy about mismatched twins reunited after years apart.

'Not long now,' I said. 'Someone will be over to help.'

She didn't laugh once, not even when I did, at parts of the film that were hilarious. I was sitting opposite, my back to the big window, watching her as much as her film. Because the room faces west, the blind was scrolled down and the light we sat in was bright yellow. There wasn't an ounce of air in the place.

'Are we all fine?' I was just making noise. 'Do we need to use the loo?'

She made no attempt to acknowledge the fact that I had spoken, just sat where she was, filthy and stinking to high heaven, pretending to be engrossed in the film. The honey pouring through the blinds behind me was all over the room and its trinkets. It was all over her too, accentuating the minute freckles on the bridge of her nose and on her cheek-bones, making the green of her eyes seem translucent, like seawater in shallows or rock pools. She looked for all the world like some *ingénue* being screen-tested in sepia of the classic era, conscious of scrutiny. Half an hour sitting there and she didn't speak once or look my way, not until I heard the gravel in my drive crunch under tyres.

'Thank you for coming.'

There were three of them in all: two men in plain clothes, including the last one I had spoken with, who was as ancient as myself; a second, far younger male; and a younger woman in uniform. The junior pair had, it transpired, met the girl before. I ushered them into the front room. The two men sat where I had been sitting. The uniformed woman stayed standing and asked, 'Do you remember us from last time?'

'No.'

They were terribly kind to her. How would they not be? They were all towering over her. She was very small, and by then without anybody in the world.

'The first thing for us all to do is go back over and check the house,' the older of the men said to the whole room. He held one hand out towards the girl and, to my surprise at least, she placed her own far slighter hand in his without hesitation and allowed herself to be pulled upright out of my armchair. 'Chances are your dada is at the house as we speak, and wondering where you are, and going frantic with the worry.'

The uniformed woman stepped outside before the rest of us. 'Thank you.' She was addressing a cluster of ladies gathered at my gate. 'Thank you now.'

They had seen the siren's revolving violet. It is also possible, when I think of it, that my cleaner had said something to a friend and word had spread over the bush telegraph. The officer was trying to disperse them so that both cars, mine and their unmarked one in which the girl was sitting, could slip away. Though it was no great distance to the house from which the girl had run, it was agreed that we would take the cars. I let all the others leave ahead. I rolled down my window at the gate and listened.

'Does she need anything?'

'The poor pet.'

'Has she somewhere to stop for the night?'

'You're all very good,' I said. 'Really.' I meant it. 'But I don't imagine it will come to that.' I released the handbrake and lifted the clutch to the bite. 'Go on about your evenings. Everything will be grand.'

I still think of that moment, even now, as the beginning. A good deal happened before that point, but none of it belonged to me. From my own perspective, I keep returning to that moment, when my car inched forward out of my gate and bumped onto the tarmac of the road, as the point of no return: the engine labouring upwards, my hands clammy on the wheel, the posse of ladies in the rear-view mirror, the brake lights of the other car fraying around the bend in the distance.

I knew all about that family. Everyone knew all about them: young people just returned after years out of the country and surviving out there in something resembling wilderness. Their story had been all over the local papers. There had been a lot of speculation, idle largely, and wide of the mark. I liked to think that I knew more than most. I had seen them from a distance, many times. It might be truer to say that I had observed them. Once, at their neighbour's insistence, I had tried calling and had watched them briefly from close quarters. I had done some research of my own. Soon after materializing on my doorstep, that girl would tell me far more than I cared to hear and I would come to realize how little I had known. And maybe, yes, I would in time remember more than even she could possibly have known or told me.

The close was only a half-mile farther out the road, and it took me no more than a minute to get there, but I was never more alone than in that minute or so between my gate and that close. It seemed to drag on for hours, that minute.

Only gradually did the ladies recede behind me, and when I finally rounded the long bend, their car had already parked up ahead and everyone was standing waiting for me. Beyond them, the light and shadow of the diminishing hills looked tempting.

I let the car slow naturally, on its gears, indicated towards the other side and ground to a standstill on the white line at the centre of the road, the way you would with oncoming traffic, though there was none. If I am honest, I would even say that I already felt guilty. Why? I had done nothing. I had done nothing apart from let the girl in, call the law and wait. I hadn't laid a finger on her.

2

THE GIRL'S MOTHER was not 'Helen', but Helen will have to do for now. She did have a real name. It was, once, a matter of public record. What was it, her real name? Nobody seems sure any more. There were even moments, towards the end, when Helen wasn't entirely certain herself.

'Which of you is Helen?'

A man with a beard and check shirt asked that. He was leaning on the frame of an open door, the one from the hallway into their kitchen, when he asked it. Nobody said anything. He smiled and said, 'Knock, knock,' then just stepped in, like a giant from a fairy story, to where they sat eating a cooked chicken with bare hands at the plastic picnic table she had bought to tide them over.

This was one of those moments when she scarcely recognized her name and sat as motionless as the others. She could hear them, either side of her, giggling slightly. They always shared, she knew, a running joke about her being as vague as fog. Now here she was, so miles away that everyone was gazing at her.

'I am,' she said, and stood, and put her hand forward for shaking.

This, you could say, is where it really began. The last week of April, a man in a check shirt pretending to be a door, and Helen stirred from heaven knows where to stand and stretch her hand forward the way people are expected to with strangers.

'Flood.'

Flood's hand felt huge and covered in cracks, like a cement shovel left standing weeks in sun. He had been hoping that Helen was her sister. Martina? Martina sounds about right. Flood had been hoping that Helen was Martina, from the way he was smiling down at Martina, the way men always did, and the way his face fell fractionally when Helen stood. There were, she noticed, little saucers of sweat in the armpits of his shirt. That's the other thing. It happened over the course of one blistering summer. The road up through the close was pure dust.

'We spoke on the phone.'

'We did indeed.' Flood smiled when he said that. She had called long distance twice early in the year: once to ask initially if he would consider a rent-to-buy, and once to arrange for keys. She had called from a payphone next to the laundry room in the basement of their old apartment block, with prepaid minutes. Flood's smile must have meant he didn't need reminding that they had spoken. 'That's why I asked for you.'

'We were wondering when we'd see you.'

'I meant to drop by sooner.' Every time he spoke, it appeared something else had caught Flood's attention. 'When did you get here?'

'Few days ago.'

'That's right.' Flood turned to acknowledge the others' presence. 'Marcus said he saw a big blue truck pull up.'

'Marcus?'

'Sister's youngest. I have him on night security for the time being.'

The girl's father wiped chicken grease from his hands and stood looking up at Flood and said something like, 'Paul.'

'Good man, Paul.' Flood started towards the front of the house. 'There's a couple of bits and bobs.'

The three of them walked the close: Helen and Paul and Flood. Paul looked like he wasn't entirely sure where he was. He kept squinting at the unblemished blue above them and nodding vacantly at whatever Flood and Helen were saying.

'Have you made yourselves known to Harry and Sheila?'

'In number three?'

'The very one.' Flood shaded his eyes and peered downhill towards the only other house occupied. The rest were bare breeze block, black cavities where there should have been double-glazing. A handful didn't even have slates on the roof. 'Smashing folks altogether.'

Coming back was her idea. Paul, she knew, would make that clear to Flood. There were several moments, during Flood's tour of the close, when Flood said something and Paul rubbed the underside of his nose as if he were trying to stifle a smirk. They walked; Paul drifted several paces behind and she slowed her own pace to let him catch up. They stopped to inspect something, and Paul came to a standstill to one side, hands in pockets, rocking on his heels. Whenever she asked a question, she made a point of raising her voice to try to include him.

'When can we expect other neighbours?'

'We've a few nibbles.'

'Nibbles?'

'Possible buyers. Young family like yourselves. From the midlands. Any day now.'

Flood lifted things as he spoke, arranging scraps of iron rod or plastic tubing into neat rows, as if that made any difference. His beard was copper with flecks of white in it. His arms were thick, brown. The hot sun, directly overhead, threw a little black pool in which Flood seemed to stand knee-deep. He kept shading his eyes and peering at her. He kept turning phrases that sounded comical, even when they weren't meant to be. At one point, crossing the dust track back towards their house, he asked, 'How long were you over beyond?'

'Over beyond?'

Flood nodded sideways, towards the open country on the road away from town, as if the next parish were the continent. 'In foreign parts.'

'Ten years,' she said.

'That long? The place must be unrecognizable.' Did Flood regret the last part of what he'd said? He might well have done, from the way he examined the ground between them. 'Have you been up the town?'

'Not yet.'

They stopped at the bottom of the driveway to theirs. Paul backed indoors without a goodbye. She wondered about apologizing, but Flood didn't seem that bothered.

'Nothing much to see. Handful of pubs and a filling station with a minimart. There's a film club in the courthouse one night a month, if you're interested.'

Helen laughed, openly this time. It sounded like he was asking her on a date. When she laughed, Flood blushed and tried to laugh as well, and she felt mean.

'You never know,' she said.

Flood laid one hand on the sign that read 'Show House'.

The letters were branded into a lacquered slice of oak. 'I'll leave that there for now,' he said. She hadn't forgotten that that was part of the deal. She just hadn't said so to the others. 'In case people want to look around.'

'Of course.'

'So hold on to the few sticks of furniture for the time being, if that's okay.'

There wasn't much: a coffee-table made from chrome and glass, a sleigh bed in the master upstairs, a photo in a walnut frame on the mantelpiece of some anonymous retired couple whom Martina had already christened George and Georgina.

'I quite like them. I always like other people's things more than my own.' She had assumed that Flood would know what she meant. When he said nothing, and just looked as puzzled as he did, she tried to brush it off. 'I suppose I'm odd that way.'

'They're just things, stuff I got in a discount warehouse, to take the bare look off.' Flood tucked his shirt into his jeans and pulled a cluster of keys from one of his back pockets. 'You can burn them when we're done.'

'No, I do, I like them,' she said again, and wished she hadn't. 'And it's not as if we're not glad of them.'

'When might you be in a position to complete?'

'To complete?'

'The buying end of the deal.'

'Sooner than later,' she said. She hadn't told Paul or Martina this either. 'That's the hope.'

'Good so.' Flood gestured towards a dinky caravan parked about fifty yards up the site, between the houses and the two identical apartment blocks at the top of the close which he referred to as 'townhouses'. 'Marcus will be up there from six every night.' Flood looked mortified by the name. 'Don't know where they got "Marcus" from. And pass no remarks to Slattery.' When Helen shrugged, Flood made a circle with his index finger. 'Used own this land.'

It was true what she had said. She preferred being surrounded by others' things. For days after, she replayed her conversation with Flood. For some reason she didn't fully understand herself, she had expected from him a smile of assent, not the bewildered sideways shift she'd got. Gradually, the way you do, she created a version in which Flood was mildly curious, enough to ask her what she meant. The belongings of strangers came with a history, she would tell him. The history made a kind of noise around those things. She preferred that second-hand noise to the silence of the new. It was reassuring. That was why she agreed to holding on to the show house's flotsam: the coffee-table, the bed, the couple scissored from a pensions brochure . . . That was why she held on to them all.

A door shut, of its own accord, somewhere on the ground floor. Everyone was definitely in bed. She lay for the guts of an hour beside Paul, just listening, to see if it would happen again. She stopped on the third step from the bottom and, almost embarrassing herself, asked of the darkened hallway, 'Hello?'

From the next house up there was a sound. It was like a hollow ball hopping off the chimney breast. It was so faint at first that she wasn't sure if there was a sound at all or just the memory of a sound like it. She slid a beanbag over to the bay window and knelt on it, her elbows on the windowsill. It took a while, but gradually her eyes adjusted to the dark outside, which was fairly watery anyway. The greys of the bare blocks differentiated themselves from the black of slates and windows. There was no light in the caravan. There were pools of hardened cement and chalk. Lots of weeds had sprouted up around the townhouses; ragwort mostly, but she had seen a few poppies too. Frayed tyres, a mangled aluminium ladder, shale and random scattered scraps of timber and scaffold. Hours the sound went on, or seemed to, a rhythmic thudding that was slight but still insistent enough to tremble the glass on George and Georgina in their frame. Then it just stopped. She stayed there until the enamel light that precedes sunrise had made everything vaguely visible, expecting whoever it was to emerge at any second and walk across the close. It was going to be another roasting day.

*

She posted a notice about child-minding on the community board in the supermarket halfway into town. She walked there with the girl for something for lunch and brought a card that they had made. The man at the till asked to read it first before it went up. There had been a few complaints recently about the nature of the notices.

'The nature of them?'

'What they said,' the man said, 'type of thing.' The man was being delicate. 'What they're advertising.'

There was a handful of shoppers, all queuing along the cooked-meats counter. Even so, the man served Helen first.

'These are before me.' She was pointing at the others queuing.

'You're grand,' he said. The other shoppers neither agreed nor complained. 'We'll let you go ahead.'

An opening behind the man led through to the serving side of a bar or a lounge of some description. She could see a mop, and rows of unopened minerals and tonics. The lunchtime news was warbling in the background. The silver outline of a pool table shone in the murk. The man was looking at her gazing through the door open at his back. He asked, 'Everything okay?'

'Everything's fine,' Helen said.

She told Sheila about putting the notice up in the supermarket. She told her later the same week, a morning they had agreed to go down to number three for coffee.

'You're great,' Sheila said.

'Am I?'

'You are, love. You're great.'

Sheila had her gas fire switched on, as in the depths of winter, an armchair pulled over beside it, a hanky tucked up her sleeve. Her hands had that soft paper-thin skin that elderly people often have. Helen and the girl had both bathed, to wash off some of the dust, and put on fresh shorts and tank-tops. They were sitting on a sofa in the bay alcove, as far from the fire as they could manage. There was a plate of chocolate biscuits wrapped either in green or orange foil. The girl had one of each. Sheila asked Helen, 'Are you not hungry?'

'I'm trying to lose weight.'

Sheila kept talking about Marcus. 'Super swimmer,' she said. Sheila had a soft spot for Marcus. 'Used be in the papers all the time. Harry goes way back with two of Marcus's uncles, on the other side.' She must have meant not the Flood side. 'They did a lot of deals together across the border in the war.'

'I still haven't met Harry.'

'You will. He's not himself at the moment. A bit seedy.' Sheila looked at the ceiling, which Helen took to mean that Harry was laid up in bed. 'He thinks the world of your husband.'

Paul had borrowed Harry's ladder to lift boxes into the attic, and had said what a gent Harry was. Everyone always assumed Helen and Paul were married. The girl stopped eating for a second, after Sheila said 'husband'. For something to say, Helen started describing Ute and Benedikt.

'Who, love?'

'The couple I worked for,' she said, 'over beyond.' Flood's phrase in her mouth tasted strange, but Sheila didn't seem to notice. 'That's why I left an ad in the supermarket, to get a job like the one I had with them.'

'You're great.'

She couldn't remember what that meant, to be great in the way that Sheila kept saying it. 'So are you!'

'No, you are.' Sheila was still perched out on the edge, still looking into flame that never changed shape. 'You're very brave to come back and make a proper go of it.'

*

Marcus was up in the caravan every night, without fail, from six o'clock. He arrived on a racing bike, wearing a hi-vis singlet and workmen's boots. He had spiky hair dyed peroxide. He had a golf club that he practised swinging in the dust, chipping pebbles into the townhouses when he looked too distracted for words and it was still scarcely dusk. He had a black-and-white portable television that lit up the inside of the caravan, like a sparkler inside a birdhouse.

'I should bring him up something.'

She was standing in the bay window of the front room. The room had nothing of theirs in it except two beanbags and a forty-two-inch screen. Paul and Martina were just back from work in the software plant on the ring road, still in their suits, and somewhere behind.

'Bring what precisely?' Martina asked.

'I should bring Marcus up some biscuits or something.'

'Leave Marcus to me. I'll take care of Marcus.'

'I bet you will.' Helen had followed them into the kitchen, was slouched in one of the other chairs and peering wide-eyed over the rim of her coffee mug. There was no food cooking. Paul had a bicycle clip on the right leg of his slacks; Martina still had her runners on, laces undone.

'Bet I will what?'

'Take care of Marcus.'

'Well . . .' You could never fully tell with Martina. She took in her stride every different thing with an ease, a lightness, that could feel the same every time. 'Poor Marcus, on his own in his little caravan every night.'

They walked to the pictures, herself and Martina. They turned left at the end of the close, passed the supermarket facing the church and crossed straight through the roundabout for the ring road. That was the first time they went up the town. Two streets, five pubs, a Chinese takeaway, a filling station with a minimart, a hardware shop. There was nobody else around. The cinema was just what Flood had said: a courthouse at the far end of the main street that screened old films on the same night of every month.

A chap with lip-piercings and a circular hole in one of his earlobes ripped their two tickets in half. They squeezed into a double seat, one row back from the very front. They had always shared a double seat as children. The film had already started, the credits, the music. Martina had brought a giant bag of popcorn that she seemed scared to eat for fear of the noise her eating would make. She set the bag across the dip created by their touching legs and linked her arm into Helen's.

'There's nobody else here.'

'I know,' Martina said. Helen was telling her not to worry about the noise. 'Still.'

There was a family of three in the film, taking care of a hunting lodge in the wilderness through the winter months. The nearest life to them was the ranger's office on the other side of the state. Vast white drifts were mounting against the outside walls and doors.

'Snow!' Martina whispered. 'Looks to die for.'

All the corridors, all the floors, were empty. A boy on a tricycle kept speeding down them, around corners, the racket of the tricycle's wheels on bare boards alternating with the carpet's silence. You could hear the reels turning. You could all but hear the column of vivid dust swirling above their heads. Several times they jumped at once. When the boy jolted to a standstill at twin girls in blue dresses, some of the popcorn got sprayed beneath the row of seats in front of them.

'Jesus!'

The twins spoke in unison, their voices distorted electronically. The piercings guy who had ripped their tickets was slouched in the back row and laughing out loud at parts that were not meant to be funny, even at the part when a man kissed a woman who turned to decomposing flesh in his arms. They watched the credits to the very end, down to the symbols and logos of bodies responsible for funding for the film, until the house lights faded up and the screen scrolled back into its case and the space was just a courthouse once again.

They called for a drink at the lounge belonging to the supermarket, the one opposite the church halfway out from town, on what locals called 'the old road'. There was just the two of them and a row of regulars at the counter. Martina asked, 'Have you heard anything back from the von Trapps?'

The von Trapps was what Martina called Ute and Benedikt, though she had never met them. Helen had emailed Ute to say they had arrived and settled in. She had mentioned to Martina that she had written.

'Nothing back.'

When it was Helen's shout, Martina rested a flat hand over the rim of her glass. A man on a high stool at the bar, well spoken and butty, insisted on paying.

'I insist,' he said. 'I knew your family.' He held a crisp twenty between two fingers and wafted it across the bar and informed the barman, 'For our new neighbours.'

'Sorry,' Helen said. She said it to Martina, resting the glasses on their table. 'You have the midget up there to thank.'

Martina raised hers to him, smiled and nodded silent thanks. She said, 'I'll pretend to drink it,' and let her lips touch the rim. It wasn't like Martina, abstinence wasn't.

'Are you pregnant?'

'I wish! I promised Marcus I'd drop up, and I don't want to be plastered.'

Martina had gone walkabout a few evenings, but never

said where she was going. The idea of her wandering up to Marcus made Helen feel safe in a way that she didn't understand. So did the thought of her sister wishing she was expecting. 'You've already made yourself known to him, so?'

'Didn't I say I would?' Martina leaned forward again and this time actually lapped from the head of her second pint. Martina had this cat-that-got-the-cream expression which always wound Helen up. She had it then. 'He's lovely.'

'He said he knew our family.'

'Marcus?'

'Not Marcus,' Helen said. All roads were leading to Marcus in Martina's head. 'The wee chap at the bar who bought the drinks.'

'Did he say anything else?'

Martina went to get change for the pool table. She was up there a good five minutes, the lad behind the bar teasing her about her cue action and the row of regulars chiming in. Playing was Martina's idea. It was Martina who rested the coins into their slots and held the tongue in until the rack was clear, who placed the balls into the triangle frame, who asked the men if they went in any particular pattern. Martina seemed to love them gawking, especially when she missed the white ball altogether and they cheered. Martina never had to watch her figure. The barman came around and stood behind her and held it for her and got her to position her hands on top of his and showed her how. Helen finished her second pint and sipped at the one Martina had no intention of drinking, situating her lips to fit the crescent Martina's lipstick had left.

How easily Martina belonged. Even when she was present only through others, she always fitted in. Why was

Martina even there? That was the question that Paul used hiss in foreign dark, with just a thin partition between them and the living room where Martina and the girl slept top-to-toe on a fold-out sofa bed. Everywhere they went Martina went as well. When it was just the two of them, Paul made it sound like he couldn't stand Martina's presence. But when Martina was there, at the table eating or chatting in front of the telly, it always felt as if Paul and Martina were on the same side and Helen was their running joke. She had tried to say to them about the noise from things that once belonged to others, which she wished she had said to Flood. They just giggled, 'If you say so,' and changed the channel. She was sorry she'd said anything, because of the way they reacted and because she realized it wasn't true. The things of a show house belonged to lives that should have happened but never did. They gave off no noise at all, and that was more deafening than anything.

'Will we make shapes?'

Martina was standing above her, with a bottle of carry-out wine in a plastic bag that had blue-and-white stripes sticking to the bottle's condensation. It had gone eleven, but some light was left and it was still plenty hot. On the half-mile of hard shoulder, Helen was telling Martina the old-fashioned phrases Flood used whenever he called.

'He's sweet on you.'

'Flood?' Helen asked, out of breath. Martina was forever doing this, telling Helen about men who liked her, resting all emphasis on the second person. 'Good God.'

'Marcus is the same,' Martina said. 'Full of ancient little turns of phrase.'

They stalled at the end of the drive. The light was on in

the caravan. Helen knew that Martina wasn't coming into the house and yet, for something to say, she said, 'You're heading up?'

'I am.'

'So be it,' Helen said. Then she asked something out of the ordinary, something that surprised even herself. 'Do you ever wonder about Mammy and Daddy?'

'What do you mean?'

'Just that. Do you ever wonder where they are?'

Martina came right up against her and kissed her very slowly on the forehead. It had been a long time. Martina smelt of coconut. She could almost feel Martina sipping tiny beads of sweat off her skin. Martina asked if she would be okay. Then Martina said, 'You need to do something.'

'Same old shit,' Paul whispered. Paul whispered that on the same night Helen came back from the pictures alone. They had three times as many rooms, and Martina wasn't even in the house, but still Paul acted as if they were in the old apartment where hushed pillow talk was the only privacy available to them.

'I'm sorry,' Helen said out loud. Paul was in bed when she got back, but still awake, still whispering. He had asked her what had kept them. Helen had told him about the lounge and the pool table and the midget at the bar who said he knew the family.

'Why is she even here?' This was his old refrain, why Martina followed them wherever they ended up, though it had been months since either of them had broached the subject. Mostly, Martina's presence was taken as read. 'Everywhere we go, she goes too.'

Helen had her head sideways on her pillow, facing away. She could feel one of Paul's legs slide between both of hers. She could feel the tip of his tongue making spirals around that ball of bone at the top of her spine.

'She gets scared,' she said, turning onto her back. She meant Martina.

'She has no imagination. She's incapable of imagining a life of her own. So she piggybacks on ours.'

'Maybe she's in love with you.'

She said that every time they had this conversation. She said that because it always seemed that Paul had instigated the conversation to hear her say it. She coaxed him up on top of her, hooking her feet together and trying to pull him farther into her. She rested her hands on either side of her head, like when you're surrendering, and he propped his on hers so that the small dull ache was the only point their torsos touched.

'In love with me? Martina?' His breath was thickening. Whenever they made love, they often seemed to talk about Martina at the same time. 'What are you on?' Or was it the other way around? Was it that whenever they talked about her sister in bed, they ended up doing it? 'She's too much in love with herself to be in love with anyone else.'

'Be careful.'

They'd met their first year at university. Helen was pregnant by Christmas and dropped out. She'd promised herself that she would go back, but never did. Paul was Helen's only ever lover and this was the only way she knew. They never used contraception. He would just withdraw at the last second. Paul was slight and no weight on top of her. He supported himself on his arms, as if he were doing push-ups, and his eyes gradually glazed. At the last second, his features seemed to puddle, just beneath the surface of fresh water. At that precise moment, it hurt. It hurt her to think that some day he would stop, or she would stop, and they would never see one another again or speak or touch. Some day, after all they'd been through together, one of them would turn and move away and not come back ever, and the other would fill the remainder of their days circumnavigating the empty space left behind.

He disappeared into the en-suite, made one tap whistle, returned to the bedroom and lay on his back with his damp hand holding Helen's. The bedroom, even with the window open as wide at it would go, was stifling. Paul was quickly dead to the world. Helen kicked their one cotton sheet to the end of the bed.

She wondered how it would be with a heavy man lying on top of her. How would that feel? A man of Flood's stature, say. The furnace of him. His bulk, too great to support itself, pressing straight down on top of you. The bristle on your cheek and the soft groaning right there at your ear. The safety, the security, of how that must have felt, to have a huge frame squeezing every ounce of air from your lungs, the pain of being completely full and pinned to a spot, mumbling his name again and again until that word's solitary syllable broke its banks and overflowed and made one lake of several outlying fields.

'There's someone banging on the door.'

They were woken by banging. Or, rather, Paul had been woken by banging and shoved Helen until she was conscious enough to see him standing at the end of the bed.

'What time's it?'

'There it is again,' Paul said.

That was the one time Paul looked scared. He struggled into his cycling shorts, which had been lying on the floor on his side of the bed. Helen heard his footfalls on the varnished stairs, his eventual muttering, the chain, the lock snicking open, and Martina down in the hall complaining that her key wouldn't turn.

'Your sister. Taking care of Marcus.'

He said that last bit with a tone. He was, the tone meant, repeating the precise phrase of a joke in which Helen had shared.

'I'll kill her,' she said.

'Can it wait till morning?'

'That was really scary.'

'You put it on the snib,' Paul said.

'The what?' It was years since Helen had heard anyone use that word. She knew what it meant. She just wanted to hear him say the word again.

'The snib,' Paul said. 'You put the front door on the snib.' He turned to face the wall on his side of the bed. 'There's nobody else in the house, love. This has to stop.'

The weather held. She kept expecting to wake to grey and drizzle, for the dust on the close to turn to muck. If anything, the mornings got clearer and hotter. Martina was always the first to leave. Paul cycled, left later and arrived before Martina. Helen breakfasted in shorts with the back door open, so that a little of the cool of the garden's shade might come indoors. The girl slept in or sat eating cereal on one of the beanbags in the front room, headphones plugged in, the keys of her laptop clicking.

Afternoons were spent unpacking and breaking up boxes for the green bin and keeping the house presentable in case any viewers came. Sometimes, distracted by the heat and by the absence of anything happening on site, Helen and the girl slipped into flip-flops and wandered. Theirs was sandwiched between two shells of houses. The shell to their right, the one farther up the close, was like their own inside out. Above the hearth someone had painted rough concentric circles in different colours, like a target, a bright red disc at the centre. The kitchen sink had a sheath of aquamarine protective contact that the girl pinched at the corner and peeled halfway across the drainer. The row facing theirs was even less finished. No doors, windows or wiring. The façades were still bare block, the roofs just timber strips and felt. They leaned in one of the front bays and could see all the way through the partition and the kitchen to the hill of long, singed grass. Beyond that, in the distance, against a deep blue sky, were horse-chestnuts in leaf and a cluster of chimney stacks.

'Herr Slattery.'

'I presume . . .' Helen said.

'Rich?'

'I believe so.' Helen could feel her shoulder blades burning. 'But from what nobody knows.'

There was no grass on the patch that Flood referred to as 'the green area'. It was just rubble, cubes of foam packaging that appliances must have come in, offcuts of yellow rubber piping and cement lumps in the shape of oil drums that neither of them could budge.

Marcus's caravan was locked. It had a sticker of the Confederate flag on the door, a row of medals strung along the window at the end, between the paled-out back of closed curtains and plastic glass hot from the glare of the mid-afternoon sun. When Helen stood on blocks and shaded her eyes, she could see fragments of the interior through gaps where the curtains didn't meet. It felt weird to think of Martina in there most evenings. She could see a wire coat-hanger sticking upside-down out of the portable. She could see mugs unwashed on a table, one of which was probably still marked with lipstick. She could see a golf club propped against a wardrobe door. It was all bathed in tangerine, like when you close your eyes and face towards the sun.

Once, curious, they strayed into Slattery's avenue. They had been around the site too often, wandered out of the close, turned right away from town and, after a hundred yards or so, come to an avenue lined with broadleaves that cast thick, cool shadow all over the gravel and the slope's wisps of overgrown grass. It was sweltering and the climb was steep. From the gate you could see the roof. Halfway up, Slattery's house disappeared from view. At one point, a shot-gun in the distance emptied one of its barrels with a lovely dull crack that echoed and scattered rooks. They stopped only when the ground levelled off and the house reappeared in its entirety. Big windows, old brick at one end, ivied pebbledash the other. There was no life. The girl asked, 'Will we call?'

'Like this?' The girl was wearing a baseball cap that kept falling around her eyes. Helen could feel her tank-top cling-ing to the sweat on her spine. Their flip-flops, feet, were filmed in gravel dust. 'I don't think we look quite the ticket.'

'What does that mean?'

'It means that we're not dressed enough.' She often had

to explain phrases to her daughter. She often forgot that the girl had been speaking another language for two-thirds of her life. 'It means *another time, perhaps.*'

They stepped off the avenue and lay down for a while in the long grass, in the shade. There was a daylight moon, a globe of dandelion seed, directly overhead. The grass tasted of sugar. From nearby, the girl's voice asked, 'Where are your *mutti* and papa buried?'

'Somewhere near here all right,' Helen said. She had a habit of doing that, the girl, of asking questions out of the blue which were oddly in keeping with her mother's train of thought. 'I've just completely lost my bearings of the area.'

'Is there a grave?'

'There must be.'

A vehicle passed on the avenue. It sounded small, by the gentle crunch, and it was moving fairly slowly. A milk float, possibly, or something of that description. They lay still where they were, hoping they were hidden. It was like a scene from one of those ancient films, an enemy convoy too near to breathe.

'When was the war?' the girl asked, when the coast was clear.

'What war?'

'The war the lady said.'

'Sheila?' The girl must have meant the war in which Harry and Marcus's uncles smuggled across the border. 'That war? That was the last century.'

They took the shortcut home, downhill across a couple of ditches of whitethorn, a dried stream and the mountain of muck and rocks the diggers had pushed off the site.

*

'Like it,' Flood said.

Flood stopped by a few times, in passing, with little or nothing to say. There was no work happening on site, however busy he tried to seem. He was picking something up for another job, looking the place over until the night-watch clocked on at six, passing the time of day. Helen had got her hair straightened one Saturday. She did it, she said, so that people could tell herself and Martina apart. Who did she mean by *people*? It took her a second to realize what Flood was referring to.

'New style,' Flood said, pointing at her hair. 'Like it.'

Flood called the summer 'powerful'. He kept saying that and wiping one hand around the nape of his neck and squinting at the sky. The summer was powerful, and there was no word of it letting up. Flood had a way of sniggering to himself, after the fact, as if he could hear how old-fashioned what he'd said had sounded. He asked, 'Any sign of Slattery?'

'No sign.'

'If he comes down on his quad, making a nuisance of himself, you refer him to me.' Flood did a voice, as though it was meant to mimic a legal euphemism, a veiled threat. 'And Harry's gone into the hospital.'

'Really?'

'For tests, I believe.'

'Come in,' she said.

'Just for a minute.' Flood kicked his boots against the step and walked ahead of her down the hall's passageway. 'I wouldn't fall out with a drop of water while we're still allowed it.'

'What do you mean?'

'There's rationing of water coming in,' Flood said. 'Do you people not read the papers?'

She filled a mug from the cold tap and handed it to him, staying standing. He raised it to her, as if to say cheers. He drained it in one go and wiped his lips with his sleeve. He looked her up and down. He said, 'You're wasting away.'

She smiled again. It was like she was vanishing, visibly. After that, he said nothing. He just placed the mug on the table. She figured, after a few seconds, that he meant her weight: she was losing weight, diminishing in front of him. What was it Martina had said about Flood on the road home from the pictures? Flood was sweet on Helen. Had Marcus said so? Or was her sister just stirring it?

'What about that family?'

'Family?' Flood asked. You could tell by the way he said it that he knew whom she meant, that he was just buying time to think of an answer.

'The family from the midlands that you mentioned?'

'Any day now,' Flood said. He was looking across at her, as though he realized he had said the exact same thing the first time they'd met. She ran her middle finger across the nape of her neck, dragging her hair forward over one collarbone and plaiting it, like bread. Maybe he meant something completely different this time. 'Any day now.'

'What do you think?' She stepped sideways and spread one arm towards the rest of the room. She was asking him what he thought of her handiwork.

'You've acquitted yourself very nicely.'

'I've . . . ?' She could see the horror in Flood's expression, the wish that he hadn't worded it that way. It was as if the moment had a hole at its centre, the heat's precise source, and they were standing on opposite sides and staring down into it at once. Another door shut, upstairs. 'You hear that?'

'They're spring-loaded,' Flood said. 'There's a little chain in the hinge. Have you not noticed the doors shutting behind you?'

'Of course I have!'

'If you just leave them resting on the latch, they'll keep pulling.' Flood was speaking softly. He was peering a little at her. 'Might take a while, but they'll keep trying to shut until they do.'

'I thought we might have had guests.'

'Guests?'

'Other people in the house,' she said, 'apart from us. Please don't tell anyone.'

'How's herself? No school?' Flood was speaking past Helen to the telly's chirping in the front room.

'September. No point sending her in for the last month and a bit.'

'We won't say anything, will we?' Flood called through. Then he said to Helen, as if the girl wasn't there at all, 'Sure she hardly says anything to anybody.'

Harry died. He went in for tests and never came out. They went down for the removal. It was late in the afternoon, and Paul and Martina were still at work. Helen and the girl rang the doorbell before the coffin was carried out. Someone they had never seen before answered. They asked for Sheila. Sheila looked gorgeous when she came out, in a black one-piece with a gold chain and matching earrings. Her lavender scent, when she embraced them both at once, was the same as Helen's mother used wear. Because of all the oil drums and muck parched to sand, the cortège had to start from the bottom of the close. Flood was among them, waiting in a slate-grey suit. Several of the mourners were holding golf umbrellas as parasols, as if they were in a procession in the tropics. Helen and the girl stood, hands crossed the way they had seen others do when praying, until the coffin was carried out and down to the hearse.

It was that night, the night of Harry's removal, when the girl screamed. That night, or the night immediately after. It was near eleven. Helen was in the bath and the girl screamed, 'There's someone in the garden!'

'What, now?'

Helen climbed out of her lukewarm suds, wrapped herself in a beach towel and went into the second bedroom, where the girl was standing at the window. Against their rear wall was a pale thumbnail that might well have been a face staring up at them. They ran downstairs. Paul was at the patio door, trying to peer through his own reflection, flicking the switch of the outside patio light.

'Nothing works,' he was growling. 'Why does nothing fucking work?'

She switched off all the lights indoors so that the inside dark merged with the dark of the garden. Paul rattled the handle of the patio door half-heartedly, thumped on the double-glazing, but the face stayed where it was. She turned all the lights back on, ran up to the caravan and rapped on its thin door with her knuckle.

'Come in,' Marcus's voice called.

Marcus was seated, one knee drawn up to his chest. Martina stood in the square yard of floor space in a bikini top. 'Hello there,' Martina said, as if her sister were someone she kind of knew from work. Martina had her arms roped around herself. She was shivering.

'Hello back.' The inside of the caravan smelt of something resembling disinfectant. She felt suddenly self-conscious, having nothing around her except a wet towel. She said, 'Excuse the intrusion.'

Marcus had been watching *Lost*. He had seen nothing. She could hear her own raised voice saying how she couldn't see the point of Marcus being paid to watch *Lost* in a caravan while all that shit was going on around them on site.

'All what shit?' Marcus had stood out of his seat. 'If you have a problem with the way I'm performing my duties, then you should speak to my uncle about it.'

When Martina shouted, 'You're being rude,' which of them was she shouting at?

'Otherwise,' Marcus snapped, 'I'll bid you goodnight.' He pushed the inside of the caravan door with the toe of his steel-capped boot so that it swung outwards, flimsily, on its hinges. Helen ran back down to the house to find Paul scrabbling for a hammer, the only tool they possessed, under the sink.

'Where the hell,' she asked, 'do you think you're going with that?'

'Round the rear access.' Paul's voice was shaking. 'Sick of this.'

The black was impure. It wasn't the black you get in winter, which is so absolute as to sparkle. This was the virtual black of a May that was almost over and was already the hottest in recorded history. The black was grainy, fraying with greys and pinks at the edges, like darkness that someone had captured on video. When Paul materialized at the back gate, he had the hammer cocked shoulder-high and was taking long, slow steps. He looked a bit of a clown, like something out of a cartoon: to Helen, a beach towel knotted around her and her wet hair combed back; to the girl, who was at her mother's shoulder and still had headphones around her throat; to Martina, who had put on a sweater and followed her sister back down to the house.

'Nothing,' he shouted. 'Not a sinner.' Helen unlocked the patio door, stepped out onto the warm cement and told Paul to come back in. 'I wanted to find something. Someone.'

'I know what you mean,' she said. What did he mean? Did he mean that nothing there, and nothing there repeatedly, was the biggest fear of all? Still gripping the knot of her towel, she held out her free hand to him. 'Please come in.'

That was more of it. The light not working on the patio, the outline of a face at the end of the garden, the rooms too hot to get a proper night's sleep. She thought that she could even hear cicadas. There couldn't have been cicadas anywhere near. It must have been just a memory from their previous life, of the noise of cicadas from forests all around the apartment complex, that millions-deep, deafening chorus.

Paul said to lie on. It sounded like he was getting dressed when he said it. He knew she hadn't slept much in the night, he was mumbling, and there was nothing that needed doing. She heard the door slam, his bike whirr down the close.

For twelve years Helen had looked on from the fringes of Paul's life, his college peers and his work colleagues. However much he tried to include her, from the moment the girl was born she experienced the parties in basement flats and wine-bar Christmas bashes with all the sadness of a revenant. She was always there and not there. She could see and hear everything, but her own words never seemed to land on the far shore and she drifted through those rooms with invisibility's weightlessness.

The girl called up that it was almost noon. They walked in single file. The automatic door of the supermarket didn't open. There wasn't even a reflection. What had been Flood's phrase? *Wasting away*. Only when the girl arrived, ten paces behind, did the door's two halves slide apart.

'Will there be,' a woman behind the counter asked, 'anything else?'

'Excuse me?'

'Anything at all?'

The road home was hot and depopulated, as if the whole world was observing a siesta. The only noise was the gravel beneath their sandals. That and the grating scream of steel being cut in the distance. The girl ate on her beanbag, speaking into her laptop's screen. Its drum-beats and distortions, its frequent high-pitched shrieks, like a courtyard with a peacock hidden in it, could be difficult to bear. The volume of the telly was up as far as it would go. That was on top of the cacophony of appliances in standby mode, the spring-loaded chains in the doors slowly forcing themselves shut.

Even the colours in the photo of George and Georgina on the mantelpiece seemed loud: the mauve of her blouse, his sweater's canary yellow, their white teeth, the sea's sapphire, the solitary smoking peak behind them, the streaks of evening vermilion. At the precise moment the shutter fell, George was speaking and Georgina was laughing at whatever he was saying. His lips were shaped around a vowel, her eyes half closed, her head leaning back.

'Oh, now.'

Their father used say that. Whenever he arrived first at the conclusion of some yarn and was waiting for the others to catch up, he would roll his fingers on the arms of his armchair and sigh, 'Oh, now.'

Outside, the bricks of their drive felt almost too hot for her bare feet. She could all but hear the earth cracking, the breeze blocks creaking under their own weight, the braids of fibre-optic cable suffocating underground. The close was a morgue. Sheila's front room wobbled with artificial flame. No cars on the road. The supermarket, in passing, looked deserted. Somewhere out beyond the immediate horizon was light traffic, like the inner storm of a seashell pushed hard against the ear. Oh, now. The phrase kept buzzing in her head. Oh, now, oh, now . . .

The ring road's hard shoulder had tar dyed red. The only other souls about were two figures, walking as well, some distance behind. However much she tried to pick up speed, they seemed to have gained with each glance back. A man and a woman, treading the shimmer, appearing airborne even. The chrome logo of the software plant where Paul and Martina worked was blinding with the reflection. In there, somewhere, whichever way you looked at it, were both her other halves. One vehicle beeped. At her, or at the couple in her slipstream? They were getting louder behind her, their steps and chatter.

The big gates, when she reached them, had a handmade sign tied to them saying the black gloss was still wet. The first headstones were grey and worn; those farther in were newer, more polished; farther still was all plastic grass and bouquets, unconsecrated scrub and thistle. Who were they beckoning? Her footfalls were being overtaken by their echoes. If not her, then who were they calling?

'Where's your mam?'

Paul was home ahead of Martina. That was how he explained it later on. He got home ahead of Martina and found all the windows wide open, the front door ajar and his daughter before the telly with a mini-screen in her hands. He said that she pulled a headphone away from one ear and shrugged quizzically, as if asking him to ask again.

'Your mam?'

He remembered leaving his bike in the hall. He came back downstairs within seconds, still sleeved in sweat from the cycle ride in his suit.

'Did she go out?' He said it was like talking to the blank walls. Lifting one headphone off his daughter's ear, he heard himself barking, 'Did your mother go out for something?'

3

Dear Ute (and Benedikt and Sophie!)

We have never met, but I feel as if I already know all of you loads! I am the sister of Helen, your former nanny. Perhaps Helen spoke about me at some point. I hope you are all well and that Sophie is enjoying kindergarten.

One afternoon a week ago, Helen went out and didn't return. Myself and her husband Paul were both at work. When we got back Helen was gone, and nobody has seen or heard from her since.

I have been writing around to everyone Helen knows, to ask if they have heard anything. Have you? I know how badly my sister missed all of you after we moved home. She mentioned that she had written to you recently. I have even wondered if Helen went back. She loved your flat and described it so often to me. Whenever I imagine her still alive and safe, it is in your lovely home. If you know of anything that might be helpful, please do get in touch.

Forgive me for writing in English. Forgive me, too, if you are the wrong people. I never knew my sister's employers' full names, only their first names and their occupations. I found you on the internet.

Thank you for reading this!!

Martina (Helen's sister) ox

'Still no word?' Flood had pulled up to the end of their drive. He had his window down full, his shirt sleeves rolled up. The engine of his banger was revving.

'Still no word,' Martina said.

'That's a terror.'

Martina was out the front, brushing dust that had blown in from the rest of the site, fighting a losing battle. The hot spell had wrung every ounce of moisture out of the muck. Flood's car was covered in it. Even Flood himself, when he climbed from the car, seemed coated in dust. Cleaning was one of several odd offshoots of Helen's disappearance. Martina had become house-proud in a way that she had never been before. Of the two sisters, it was Martina who had always been the slob.

'She'll show up.'

This was Flood's usual tack: Helen would show up, one day soon, out of nowhere. With houses still to flog, Flood was determined to put an upbeat spin on what had happened. Martina, on compassionate leave to mind the girl, had seen more of Flood in the past fortnight than she had in the month before that. The sun was directly overhead, so that the shadows they cast were minimal.

'Uncle of mine was gone ten years. Ten years! They found his body in the Thames, shipped it home, buried him. Not five miles from here.'

Martina had heard the story about Flood's uncle. Twice before from Flood, and once from Sheila, who said it had been all over the papers at the time. 'Really.' Martina wanted to say that she had heard it. She wanted to tell Flood to take a running jump. But that wasn't how she and Helen had been brought up.

'Then his two daughters won tickets for *The Phantom of the Opera*. They were stood in an Underground train on the way to the show when one of them heard her name being said behind her. Who was there when she turned around?'

'Go away . . .'

'The man himself.' Flood was shaking his head. 'The divil knows who they buried.' You'd swear Flood was hearing his own story for the very first time. 'She'll show up yet.'

'Any sign of this tar?' According to Flood, if you mentioned Flood to Slattery, Slattery bolted. You mentioned the promise of tar to Flood and you saw his face glaze, his watch twitch. She said, 'It's like the desert here.'

Flood was shifting backwards towards his car. 'You have the flip-flops and togs. All you need is a beach towel around your neck.'

Helen would never have gone to London. Helen and Paul had spent three months there, the summer before his last year at university. She'd hated the stickiness of it, the proximity to home, the way that you felt always within earshot of news. She hated most of all the Sundays there, the jarred familiar accents on buses, the desolate municipal playgrounds you went to with your little daughter, the brass of some Salvation Army band on the corner of a half-open shopping precinct that would make you want to run howling into the nearest hills.

Martina had told all this to the officers in the first few days. There was no way that Helen would have gone there. Martina said that they had no family to speak of. Did Helen have any close friends Martina knew of whom she might have gone to? Martina said that she and Helen were best friends.

'After Mammy and Daddy,' she said, 'we just stuck together.'

She had felt her face reddening when she said that. She wasn't certain if that made her look embarrassed, about to cry or both.

'Could I ask you to take your daughter into the front room?' the female officer said to Paul. 'We'd like to address a few questions to Martina, alone. Is that okay?'

'Okay,' Paul said. He let the girl slip through ahead of him. 'Sounds worrying.'

Martina had scrunched a face of bemusement, if only to say that she had no clue either. They made sure that the partition door was closed properly. The female officer said, 'How would you characterize your relationship with Helen's husband?'

'Paul?' She had said his name softly, so that it wouldn't be audible in the front room. 'They aren't married.' She glanced between them, both looking straight at her, waiting for an answer. 'What do you mean exactly?'

'Martina, we're not here to judge.' The officer's voice had come with a trained kindness, an off-the-record intimacy that they must all have learned. 'We have lives of our own. We do understand how things can go.'

'No,' she said. Her way of clipping that came over every bit as horrified as she felt. 'Paul is my sister's husband. He and I . . .' She heaved an angry, protracted sigh. 'Just because I've lived with them . . .' She all but scoffed at the officers, with their studied familiarity, their residual acne and their questions copied from evening drama. 'Never.'

Martina and Paul had both sat in while the officers interviewed the girl, the last one to have seen Helen. Was there anything in particular about that day that she could remember? Anything at all that seemed unusual? When the girl spoke, she looked at her father for correction or reassurance. After every natural stop, Paul looked up at the others to make sure they had understood. She and her mother had walked to the supermarket to buy rolls and sliced ham for lunch. They had both eaten out the back, in the sun. Her mother had said it was too hot and gone in to get a hat. After that, the girl couldn't remember very much. She had gone inside herself, for a while, to watch telly. She couldn't remember seeing her mother from that point onwards. Next thing she knew, in fact, her father was home and very flustered.

The officers had asked for a recent photo. Paul emptied a plastic tub of photos onto the floor. He looked small and sad down there, on his knees on the polished boards, sliding pictures around with his hands. He looked, Martina thought, like the little boy he must once have been, sorting his Top Trumps cards.

Forty-eight hours. That was what they said. Over ninety per cent of missing-persons cases got resolved within forty-eight hours. Within a week, a close-up of Helen – squinting, lakeside, Martina's arm visible around her shoulders like an ermine collar – was on posters everywhere.

You never know how you might react until it happens. The odd thing is, nobody cried. Or, at least, Martina could remember none of the others crying. She had, initially, to herself, in the spare room. But Paul seemed too intent on looking after his daughter, and the girl seemed too wrapped up in whatever screen was before her. After the authorities and the posters, after several articles in provincial papers and a brief notice in one of the nationals, nobody said anything really. Martina didn't want to upset them by continually talking about her sister, but kept hoping that Paul or the girl would. When nobody did, it occurred to her that maybe their reticence was out of consideration for her. Maybe, as a form of kindness, they were waiting for Martina to raise it. Gradually, a dazed, muted normality reconvened, in which Helen's disappearance went weirdly unmentioned.

Maybe the really odd thing was Paul occasionally calling his daughter Helen. At first it was just a mistake, that commonplace parent's slip of the tongue. The girl stopped correcting him. She seemed to like being called by her mother's name. She said so and Paul forgot that he was mixing them up. Even Martina, who could see how weird it was, called her Helen on a couple of occasions as well. Sometimes that was the only way you could get the girl's attention. Other times it felt like keeping Helen, the real one, nearby.

She surfed nights on sites for missing persons. This was some people's world, belonging to a family member who had disappeared, keeping one another afloat with the Xs of strangers' chatroom kisses and groundless hope. It was one of those nights, prompted by the officers' questions, that she wrote to Ute. The Ute she found, the one most likely to fit the bill, was under 'Features' with the state broadcaster. It wasn't true what Martina had said in the email, that she had been writing around to all the people Helen knew. There was nobody else to write to.

Martina and the girl sunbathed out the back. The days were still cloudless, searing. They rose late, long after Paul had left, ate muesli on beanbags in front of some chat-show or antique weepie, tidied around the kitchen and basked away the rest of each day on beach towels on the patio. There was no work happening on site. By early afternoon, the sun had moved around to the back of the house and cast the slatted shadows of fences across the garden's parched muck.

Most afternoons Marcus would text, asking when he was going to see her again and why she had stopped visiting at nights. He addressed her, in every text, as 'babes', which made her feel ancient. It was, indeed, possibly the very first thing ever to make her feel ancient. The endearment post-dated her: she had never known anybody call anybody 'babes'.

'Who was that?' the girl would ask.

'Nobody.'

'Again?'

She gently pressed a finger on her niece's nose. She said, 'Keep that out, missy.' She wasn't sure if the girl had ever realized about herself and Marcus, and she would have been mortified by the idea of trying to explain. She kept her phone on vibrate on the counter top in the kitchen, so that its drone was loud and unmistakable even when she was out in the sun.

'There's nobody also!' The drone had become unmistakable to the girl. 'What must he want?'

'Nothing.'

'You're not texting back?'

'Very little credit. Nosy!'

Martina took redundancy at the software plant. Her boss, given the circumstances, negotiated a minuscule package on her behalf. She bought creepers and trellis wire for the back wall. She bought sun-loungers in the discount supermarket off the ring road. They walked there: two miles max, and yet she had to drag her niece by the hand for the last bit. They both wore baseball caps and were drenched with sweat by the time they arrived. The supermarket's inside seemed black at first. Its air-conditioned temperature came as a relief. Once their eyes adjusted to the indoor murk, they could see that the produce wasn't shelved. It was just piled high on pallets you had to climb up onto to pull things down. Some of the 'Special Offer' signs hanging from the ceiling were in a language neither of them recognized or could decipher. All the food came in wrapping that looked off-colour, in brand names that sounded fractionally to one side of what you would expect. The sun-loungers were flat-packed, down at the end. She got a trolley, squeezed two of the loungers into it, and phoned for a minicab. They sheltered in the porch, until someone shouted, 'Martina,' from out there in the glare. She gave him a ten, though the fare was nowhere near that, and said not to bother about the change. He asked her, 'Are you not the lassie who went walkabout?'

'Who went . . . ?'

'Walkabout.'

'Walkabout?' The girl started giggling and Martina had to nudge her several times across the back seat. The driver must have read about Helen in the paper. 'Am I not the lassie who went walkabout? I am of course! Just over here, thanks. We'll go walkabout from here.'

'You're welcome back.' He winked into the rear-view mirror, as if he was equally in on the joke.

'You're very good,' she said.

The driver insisted on hauling the boxes from the boot. He gave her the card of his minicab firm.

'Ask for Dermie, and Dermie'll be there in a jiffy.'

'Let me guess. You wouldn't be Dermie by any chance?'

'No flies on you!'

Dermie was five nothing, a navy anorak fading at the elbows that smelt of the inside of his cab. He asked if the girls would manage to assemble the sun-loungers. Martina had to apologize for her niece. 'Something else,' she said. 'Private joke. You're as good.'

Dermie shouted up to them, from the driver's door, 'I'd kill to see you stretched out on one of those.' He was gesturing at the boxes. He meant the sun-loungers. He meant Martina. She waved and muttered that his name sounded like a skin disease.

She went topless. They had always gone topless before. Everyone did. Paul was at work all day, the girl accepted her going topless as second nature, and it wasn't as if there were many neighbours to scandalize. She had a bright silk scarf that she knotted across herself as a bikini top in case there was the stir of someone else around or Flood rang the doorbell, which he hadn't done in a while. Marcus didn't get there until six. They had the place to themselves all afternoon. The girl could be nervous. More than once she was convinced that she saw something flitting between the fences that partitioned the rear gardens. How could she not be nervous, after everything that had happened? Martina, as was always her way, made light of the shadows. She did it for her own sake as much as for anyone else's, but you would never have guessed that.

'Probably just Dermie,' she would yawn. She talked

about Dermie as if they were lovers and wedding bells weren't far off. 'I told him to come around the back if there was no answer.'

'In his anorak?'

'Hope so. I love a man in an anorak.'

Slattery too. Slattery was their other phantom. Any peculiar happening or sound was blamed straight away on Slattery or on Dermie or on both of them. A gate unbolting down the way, or a call that was dead by the time Martina could press 'answer', was Dermie or Slattery. Or, when things got particularly silly after a day pickling in the screaming sun, it was George and Georgina, still on the mantelpiece and spoken of like elderly relatives Martina did messages for. Or it was all of them at once, sniffing around the margins like a pack of dogs.

'I don't care who sees,' she said once. 'They can have a good peep for all I care.'

'That's what *Mutti* said about you.'

Martina pushed her sunglasses back onto her hairband, propped herself on her elbows and shaded her eyes. The girl hadn't mentioned her mother once since her disappearance. She was smirking when she said that, or seemed to be. Not meanly, more teasing. Martina could hardly see her since the sun was directly behind her head. She was a silhouette, a blind spot, an eclipse. She seemed to be sitting upright, head bowed, playing with beads or something between her legs.

'What did your *mutti* say about her darling sister? Tell me.'

'She said that you loved being gawked at.'

It was true. Martina knew it was true that Helen had said

that from the word the girl used. 'Gawked' was pure Helen. Or, rather, it was the kind of word Helen had loved using. The longer they'd spent over beyond, the more Helen sprinkled her conversation with quaint words that their father would have spoken, that had made her homesick and eventually a little sweet on Flood.

'That's what your mam said? That I like being gawked at?'

'That you *love* being gawked at.' The girl shaded her own eyes and turned her face up to the dome of azure.

'The cheek of her.' Martina said it to let the girl know that it was okay, that she was forgiven, that Martina thought it was funny. 'I'll be ancient long enough and nobody will want to gawk at me then. I might as well enjoy it while they do.'

Paul's mother and father visited, just for the day. The mother didn't take off her coat once. Deep red, woollen, it stayed buttoned to her throat all afternoon. The father had trailered a few bits that had lain untouched in Paul's old room: a dog-leg computer desk, a filing cabinet painted grey gloss, a giant chrome-plated fan. Paul and his father carried them into the front room. Paul, knowing his father was no longer supposed to lift heavy objects, said that he could move them upstairs piecemeal later on.

Martina put a gingham cloth on the picnic table. She asked Paul to wheel in the leather swivel computer chair that had come in the trailer. She said the two girls – she was including herself in the word – would sit on that. The rest sat on picnic chairs. Martina had asked Sheila to join them. Sheila said that it was lovely, whether or not it was.

'It makes a lovely change from packing,' Sheila said.

'Packing?' Martina asked.

'I'm moving in with my daughter. I'll probably rent below.' Sheila patted Paul's arm. 'You hold on to Harry's ladder, pet.'

'You know Sheila's husband passed on recently,' Martina said to Paul's parents. She didn't want to say 'died'. She recalled the phrase that everyone had used with them years ago, how odd and oddly acceptable 'passed on' had become, until she could hear it in her own voice there at the table.

'Ah, go on,' Paul's mother said. Martina couldn't remember Paul's mother's name. She couldn't ask, after all those years of being effectively family. 'And this was only recently?'

That was what they talked about. Harry's passing on. Sheila sniffled a little, but otherwise looked chuffed to be able to recount the details once more. Paul's father had his mouth open, speechless, all the way through. Paul's mother had one leaf of lettuce suspended mid-air on a fork. Martina and Paul were the only ones on wine. She kept trying to catch his eye, to get a refill as quietly as possible, but Paul was too caught up in the story, even though he had heard it several times. Harry 'melted'. That was the word Sheila kept using. Fit as a fiddle one day, at the doctor's the next, buried four weeks later. He just melted.

'Paul?' Martina wiggled her empty lime-coloured picnic cup in his direction. 'When you're ready.'

It was easy for Sheila, holding court like that. Everyone could listen to what she was saying without embarrassment. Harry was almost seventy-nine when he died. They had been together for over fifty years. There was a funeral that half the town came out for. Harry had had a proper send-off – one that made Sheila's stories possible.

'You never know, do you?' Sheila had her hanky out. She was dabbing the corner of each dry eye. 'Five weeks between the tests and the funeral.' Even Paul, who never seemed to notice anything he didn't have to, had stopped eating. 'He was my best friend, and he just melted.'

Martina asked if anyone fancied coffee and drilled water from a bottle into the kettle. She had the leather seat to herself after that. The telly was on in the front room. For ages it looked like nobody was going to say a thing. Sheila was too absorbed in her own performance. Paul was staring at his parents, who had the look of people who had realized it was down to them, but neither could conjure a phrase to get there. They weren't grieving in any way that was visible, and they were maybe a bit embarrassed by that. They were anxious, they kept saying, to get most of the homeward route completed before dark. It wouldn't be dark until after ten, yet they were talking as if it was November. Helen wasn't their daughter. They didn't really care that much, but had just enough gumption to make it appear that they did, if only for their granddaughter's sake.

It was Sheila who asked, 'What's the latest?'

'Very little,' Paul said. 'All we have is one possible sighting, walking on the ring road. Barefoot no less.'

Even then, his parents said nothing. They gazed gravely at the table, as if calculating how long they could reasonably leave it before heading.

'I've posted lots of notices online.' Martina was determined not to let them off the hook. 'Chatrooms, and stuff like that.'

'Of course.' Sheila clearly hadn't a clue what she was on about. 'And how will you manage?'

'I've taken redundancy. Paul will keep working, for the time being.'

'You're very good.'

Did Sheila mean Martina was accepting responsibility that wasn't really hers to accept? Martina had been dwelling on what the officers had asked her, wondering if there were rumours. She wanted to make it clear that she and Paul weren't together, an item. Once again, she hesitated until it felt too late, and then she immediately regretted that she hadn't said anything.

Maybe it was the sunbathing that was the oddest reaction of the lot, odder than occasionally calling the girl Helen. The way they took to sunbathing. The way they were, indeed, passionate about sunbathing. They bought new bikinis, discussed sunscreen factors and angles to the sun, invented their own screening and rotation system and gave it a name: 'The Spit'. Martina made it their military regime. Four sides, twenty minutes each and twenty indoors; three diminishing levels, the last and longest a weak oil with tints of bronze. It wasn't just about being brown. They called it their work. The girl loved being in charge of the timer she set on Martina's phone. 'Everybody turn,' she sang, when the timer timed down into beeps. She recorded herself and saved it as the timer alert. You knew when the electronic *Everybody turn! Everybody turn!* squeaked twice that time was up.

Martina got into the habit of drinking small bottles of rosé in the afternoon. She waited until after four, the day's regime mostly over. She wore yellow rubber flip-flops, drank from a picnic cup and drifted around the garden sipping after the girl had put on her headphones. They were out there every evening when Paul, his day's work behind him, pushed his bike through the front door. Martina thought nothing of tiptoeing around him in the kitchen, in shades and briefs, asking how all the lads at the plant were getting on. Everything looked green inside, after hours in the glare. The fitted units, the table and chairs, even Paul slumped there in his suit, they would all be lime green for a while.

'I feel like a pig,' she said. The cord of her sombrero was around her throat, and her arms were folded behind her back. 'One that's been on a spit, I mean.' Paul laughed a quiet, weary laugh, making a meal of removing his cycle clips. 'Are you okay?' She was smiling to herself, at his refusal to look up, at her sister's words spinning in her head. She loved being gawked at. She placed one finger under his chin and gently pushed his face upwards. 'Are you okay?'

She thought nothing, eventually, of giving the little one tipples of rosé, of letting her go topless too. The sun shifted sideways across each day. South-east to south-west was sunbathing prime time. They positioned and repositioned the loungers to keep facing it full on. The radio changed voices, stations. Every now and then you could hear a lorry barrelling past on the road or a car alarm warbling. A hot-air balloon crossed directly overhead late one Friday. Its stripes were orange and purple. You could make out heads leaning over the basket. Martina and the girl stood on their sunloungers, as if that made them any nearer the balloon, and whooped. After it had drifted from sight, Martina said how daft they must have looked, two naked insects waving among the half-built houses and dilapidated hardware and scorched earth. It must have been one of those afternoons, around about then, in that state, that I saw them.

They were often past giggly by the time Paul got home. Mostly, he didn't seem to know where to put himself. They would hear him, from the garden, entering the kitchen. They would call to him, but he never came out, and he could take an age upstairs to change out of his suit.

Once, and once only, Martina followed Paul up while he was changing. She tapped on the door and walked straight in without waiting to be summoned. She hadn't put on a T-shirt before coming up. She was in their room, Paul and Helen's, before it occurred to her that she hadn't put anything on. She wanted to know if they would phone out for a Chinese. Martina and the girl had been talking all afternoon about phoning out for Chinese.

'On me,' she said. She folded her arms, laughed at him for staring and asked again what he thought about Chinese for dinner.

'What is?'

It was like Paul had never seen her in next to nothing before, or any woman for that matter. It was like Paul didn't speak English any longer. He was still staring at her. Martina had on bronzing oil. Her skin was glistening with it. Her shoulders felt red and sore. Her navel was pierced with some kind of crystal stud. Her arms had freckles peppered on them. She tilted her head and, unfolding her arms, formed a rope of her falling hair.

He said, 'What's on you?'

'Food!' She sat down on the end of the bed where Paul was sitting. It was only then that she noticed he was clutching his suit trousers in his lap. She asked him, 'Are you okay?'

Red dust off the site had stuck to the oil on her skin. From the way her skin glittered, there must have been particles of mica in the dust. She had the exact same solitary mole on the underside of one of her breasts that Helen had.

'I never noticed that before,' he said. He sounded like a little boy.

'I should hope not.' Her voice was soft, like tar in hot sunlight. 'It'll be okay.'

For the first time, after weeks of keeping calm, the weirdness of it all was apparent on his features. The weirdness of what? Of his wife going missing, and her face in newspapers and on community noticeboards in shops. Of the way the world just carried on after a fashion, like a lake's surface flattening after a splash, and expected the three of them to follow. Of how the girl assumed her missing mother's name. Of how Martina's presence probably helped to bypass any grief he might have been expected to experience. Of how like his vanished wife she must have been, in the bedroom that had been theirs, almost completely naked, her black hair and green eyes, the tiny gap between her front teeth.

'Helen,' Paul said, crouching slightly forward.

'Sssh,' she was saying very softly. 'It's okay.'

He closed his eyes, squeezing them tight. 'Helen.'

'It's okay.' She couldn't think of anything else to say. She wasn't even certain what was happening. 'It's okay, it's okay.'

His breath stopped, kind of rattled, and released after several seconds. There was the smell then, like disinfectant. Martina went into the en-suite for some reason, ran the taps, sloshed suds around her hands, though she hadn't touched him at all. Paul sat there, head bowed, not moving. She shut the en-suite door quietly. She said she meant it when she'd said that it would be okay, that she would see him down-stairs. She stepped onto the landing and shrieked, 'Jesus, Helen!'

The girl was barefoot on the landing, her headphones removed. It was possible that she had been standing out there all along and met Martina emerging from the master bedroom with her hands freshly washed. Martina said, 'Your daddy's just a bit wobbly, love. I was talking to him.'

'Is he okay?'

'He's grand. Let him dress and we'll go down and pick something from the menu.'

The nearest takeaway, in town, was called the Lucky House. The woman delivering arrived in a van and shouted through the open door. It was Paul who went out. She stood there staring past him into the house, even after Paul had paid her. There was a small boy in the passenger seat of the van. The food was steaming in a brown bag. They had thrown a handful of fortune cookies on top. Martina had dressed and laid the table, and the three of them ate as if nothing was any different.

'This day has been bizarre,' the girl said.

'What do you mean?' Martina was glancing back and forth between the girl and Paul. When the girl didn't reply immediately, she asked again, 'Helen, how was it *bizarre*?'

'I saw *Mutti* in the garden.'

'Your mother? Today?'

'While you were upstairs. She walked across the garden.'

'While we were . . . ?'

'Upstairs. Talking.'

Martina and Paul waited. This, they seemed to agree, tacitly, together, at once, was the girl's way of telling them she believed something had happened. Perhaps even that she had heard. Martina, not for the first time, wanted to explain that nothing really had happened, that they had nothing to hide, but she couldn't order the words properly in her head. The girl had not really seen her mother in the garden. She was just saying the thing most likely to disturb. She was just saying something that would be certain to cause guilt.

'Okay,' Martina said. The girl had been through more than enough, and this kind of reaction was to be expected, even humoured for the time being. 'Where exactly?'

'In the garden. I was reading my magazine, and thought someone was trying to . . . I saw it was *Mutti*. She walked across the garden. I called to her, but she didn't answer. She didn't even look around.'

'And what was she wearing?' Martina asked, smiling, thinking she had finally got it and was happy to play along.

'She was wearing the bridesmaid's dress she wore at your wedding.' It was years since anyone had mentioned Martina's wedding or marriage. 'Down to the ground, bare arms, and covered all in flowers.'

Sheila moved out. She left a card in their door the day she moved. The card said 'Good Luck' in gold joined-up writing. It had a horseshoe embossed on the cover. A lamp timed on in her front room every night. There was clattering in the other empty shells. Flood came one morning and erected a metal barrier across the entrance to the close, but that made no difference. Sometimes there was hammering on their door: always at night; always the same furious rhythm, as if someone were trapped outside and desperate to get in. But there was never anyone there. Paul called to the local garda station on one of his Saturdays at home and spoke over an intercom to an uninterested voice in a bigger station in the next town. He got a heat-sensitive halogen light fitted above the patio door. It was like a disco in the garden, with the light tripping on and off. Three, maybe four, nights of every week they each lay in their separate unlit rooms, listening to the front door shuddering and joyriders buzzing like mosquitoes out on the ring road.

The water rationing intensified. The taps ran dry from eight every evening. It hadn't rained for almost two months. The mounds of muck up at the townhouses had dried to a fine orange sand that blew off in plumes whenever a warm wind came swirling around. The sand got everywhere: into the house, their clothes, everything. It got on the scraps of furniture they had, on the fruit in the picnic salad bowl. Every mug of tea or coffee seemed to have a film on its surface. You took a shower and the shower basin was coated with it, as if you had been at the beach all day. There was no point in cleaning the windows: within twenty-four hours they were gauzed with sand again.

'So be it.'

'So be what?'

Martina said it to the girl first, sitting on the edge of her lounger. Martina, for the very first time, said 'So be it' really slowly, peering above her shades, rising as she spoke. It was the girl who asked, 'So be what?'

She pointed at the patio window, until the girl slid into her sandals and stood as well. Then she stopped pointing. The words were in reverse, in a script so odd that they could have been written by a small child or someone's wrong hand.

The three words were on the outside of the patio window, so that they could be read from indoors. Someone had inscribed, with one finger, 'TI 3B OƧ' into the dust. Not recently, by the look of it. The letters had filled again, were only minutely lighter in shade than the rest of the glass and legible only from an oblique angle.

The girl asked, 'What does it mean?'

'I've no idea,' she said. 'Say nothing to your daddy.'

'Sure?'

'He has enough on his plate.'

'His plate?'

She filled a basin with warm suds and washed the window panel. A solitary sparkling panel looked dubious, so she did the rest of the panels of the patio window, and the window over the sink as well, and the bay window in the front room. She even polished them with one of her sister's old tank-tops as a rag. And yet, however hard she polished, she could never fully eradicate an impression of the words, as if the glass had memory and the letters were burned into it.

Neither she nor the girl said anything about the words, their phrase. Not then or for a long time. Not to Paul and not even between themselves. Paul never seemed to see them. Though every once in a while one of them would say 'So be it' in answer to something completely unrelated and trust that somewhere within earshot the other would hear.

Things disappeared. The cement mixer disappeared. A stack of breeze blocks diminished, almost imperceptibly, until there was nothing where it had been. A soft-top that joyriders had long since bulldozed into a mound of soil disappeared piecemeal: wheels, doors, upholstery, the instrument panel. A guy in white shorts removed the registration plates, carefully, with a screwdriver he had in his pocket. Martina watched him from the bay window. She told the others he looked as if he was the owner. Even Flood, it seemed, went missing. Where once his visits had been daily, or as good as, leaning out from the driver's window and asking for news of Helen and generally acting as if he had done them the biggest favour of their lives, now he was nowhere.

Hi, Martina! Thank you for this. I remember Helen. She came to us a few times only. But years ago, not recently. Really? We stopped her when we discovered items were missing. We worried for Sophie also. I said this to police who called lately and told us. Helen is not with us. I receive no email from her. I & Benedikt are confused. This is too sad. We will pray for you for finding her. xx

Nothing was the same. Her phone credit ran out. There was, she explained to the girl, no real point topping up. She told the girl, eventually, about the email from Ute.

'What did it say?'

'Only that your *mutti* isn't there.' There was little else she could say.

Some people appeared. A door shut upstairs. 'Spring-loaded,' the girl said, but there were definitely voices coming from the master bedroom. When another door shut, minutes after, Martina called from the foot of the stairs, threw on a jacket of Paul's off the banister and called again from the landing, her heart thumping in her breast, 'Hello?'

'Hello,' a woman's voice called from inside Paul's room. Then its door's chrome handle turned, and wire coathangers could be heard jingling on the other side. A man and a woman, both middle-aged, stood among Paul's strewn clothes.

'Do you mind telling me what you think you're doing?' Even Martina was shaken by the anger in her voice. 'Do you mind telling me who the hell you are?'

'Now hold on a sec,' the woman said.

'No harm done,' the man said.

'We did ring the bell. There was no answer and the door was open.'

'Was it?' She had the jacket wrapped tightly around herself. She wasn't even sure if the people were real. 'Leave, please.'

'Now hold on,' the woman said again. 'We were led to believe that you were still open for viewing.'

'Do we look as if we're open for viewing?'

'No harm done,' the man said again, after they had descended and stepped outside. 'I'll give Flood a ring and straighten out the crossed wires.'

Nothing ever happened about it. Flood didn't come to explain, and no other viewers appeared. Like everything else, it was never mentioned again. Then one evening at dinner Paul said that the show-house sign was gone. It could have been gone days, weeks, for all they knew. The couple viewing, along with Helen's disappearance, and Martina's thing with Marcus, and that one time in the bedroom between her and Paul, and Ute's email, and those words backwards on the patio window became a tide of unmentionables rising around them.

*

Martina started bringing things up to Marcus again. The first few times she left without saying a word, as if she were just popping up for ten minutes, and accidentally didn't get back until Paul and the girl had gone to bed. She remembered the question Helen had asked her coming home from the pictures and, after a fashion, took to calling its phrasing into the front room.

'I'm heading up.'

There was no response from inside. She winced after saying it. At least she was being honest. She was no longer pretending to be making a flying visit. She could hear the quiz that Paul and the girl loved, the answers they murmured from their matching beanbags before the contestants answered, the murmur of the fan that Paul's father had brought. She had her own answer lined up in her head if Paul ever asked her. She was going to say that she felt safe. If Paul asked, or if the girl did, she was going to say that Marcus made her feel safe at night. But neither of them ever asked.

Marcus would step out of the caravan when he saw her coming: hard hat tilted back, hi-vis singlet and nothing underneath, baggy combats and hands in pockets. His way of speaking was the match of his uncle's.

'There you are,' he would call, when she was within earshot. 'I thought I should step out to greet you.'

'You're a gent.'

Sometimes she would bake flapjacks and bring him up a plate. He liked those. He liked, as well, Helen's leftover body spray that Martina sometimes wore. He had a habit of biting and smiling at once. They sat inside the caravan, soaps on the portable. For the first few visits, they just talked. Marcus's father had died when he was small. Flood had been very good to him. Marcus was planning on going to London soon. There was nothing keeping him at home.

'Nothing at all?'

The way he went red was just like Flood, the way he blushed and snuffed a small laugh and looked at the table between them.

'Almost nothing.'

The second time Marcus said it, he pronounced 'nothing' correctly. When they were just talking, about anything, and his heart was going slow, his soft country accent cut the sharp corners off words. But if it started getting somewhere, coming to a point, he seemed to complete pronunciations properly. She knew he would never initiate anything. She came around to his side of the booth and sat on his knee. She said, 'Do you mind?'

'By all means.'

'By all means!'

When did he start using phrases like that? Trying to look educated to her! She got his top lip between her teeth and squeezed softly as if it was a strip of rubber, or squid more like. His breath tasted of instant coffee. His clothes smelt of industrial adhesive, in a sweet way. Its reek was in his skin. She went up with something on a plate, listened to him speak and sat on his knee. She never let it get too far. A lit caravan in an unfinished close was like a goldfish bowl. Midnight, or a quarter past at the latest. That was the curfew she stuck to, initially.

She didn't make much of an effort to start with. She went up in the shorts and flip-flops she had been wearing all day. A week or so of that and she changed. Jeans maybe, a nice top. The girl asked her if she was going out.

'Not exactly,' she said. 'I just have all these good clothes I never drag out any more.'

She would change before they sat to dinner, to make it seem that dinner was the reason she had changed. She had taken to serving it on paper plates, to save on washing up. She set aside one portion of whatever she had cooked in a flat sealed dish to bring up to Marcus, and stored it somewhere out of sight in case Paul asked who it was for. She was always the one who cleared the plates into the black bin bag that hung off the handle of the patio door.

She was capable, too, of seeing how they must have regarded her from their beanbags. At thirty, she was dressing up every night to go calling on a security guard just turned twenty, in a caravan on a close that was beginning to resemble some historic ruins. She wasn't only doing it, she was excited by it. The entire day had become a means of manoeuvring to this moment, when she pulled the front door in her wake and forced herself not to turn back towards the bay window.

'There you are,' Marcus would always say.

Marcus gave her golf lessons. It was the second week, possibly the third, that she had been going back up. He had mastered the art of chipping pebbles through windows and seemed determined to teach her with his one club. He had bought orange plastic practice balls, with holes in them, especially for her. She wasn't fussed, but she could see that he had gone to trouble. Marcus stood behind her, fixed her grip, kept both arms around hers and made them swing. She was missing the balls and Marcus was cheering, 'Fresh air!'

The balls were bouncing off the walls around the window's black cavity. She could feel him pressed against the back of her. She whooped when the last one disappeared.

'What happens now?'

'You have to go and get it.'

'I'm not going in there on my own,' she said.

The ground was uneven underfoot. Something scattered in one of the upstairs rooms, though there were no stairs. He was stepping backwards, holding both her hands. His felt huge and cold. It was like being blindfolded. It was like pausing at the altar steps. They stopped only when Marcus's back bumped against solid wall.

'Now,' he said, 'let's see if you can find it.'

His buttons unfastened easily. He had no underwear on. She hunkered down, not wanting to kneel and get her jeans dirty, and opened her mouth as wide as she could. She steadied herself with one hand against the vague white of his thigh, and held tight with the other to stop him from pushing too far. He kept filling his lungs in short gulps, as if surfacing repeatedly for air. He smelt, down there, of nothing other than chlorine. She could taste her own lip-gloss smearing on his skin and on her tongue. Her ankles were aching. An image of the tidal pool she and Helen had bussed to one Sunday morning, of her sister's aquamarine one-piece bathing suit, was flitting through her head. She hummed surprise. She had forgotten how young he was. She assumed that she had ages yet. It came in a cluster of waves and she concentrated on inhaling through her nose, for fear of drowning. It tasted of salt and sweat, of kelp and seawater. It tasted like a colour. Light grey. It tasted of what a mouthful of light grey must taste of.

'I'm very sorry,' he said. 'Are you all right?'

He said that in the caravan. He had made a bed of where the table had been and spread an unzipped nylon sleeping bag over them.

'I'm grand.' She was laughing, pleased it had happened so quickly. She enjoyed the suddenness, the force of it. 'It was lovely.'

She slept in fits and starts. He did several checks of the site. After each, he came back and lay around her. Once, she woke to find him standing over a boiling kettle.

'Tea.'

He lay on top of her sometime around dawn. He hadn't asked and she didn't make to stop him. His trousers were already down around his ankles. She could hear the buckle of his belt tinkling. She was bearing, she felt, all his weight. It was longer than the first time, but not by very much. The tea was strong and lukewarm.

'Where are you off to?'

'It's six o'clock,' he said. He had the strap of a rucksack across one shoulder. He was hooking the strap with his thumb. 'My shift's over.'

'Do I just lock up?'

'Just pull the door behind you.'

Evenings took the same routine. Martina had cooked before Paul got home, had changed and laid paper plates on the picnic table. Somewhere between supper and the late news, she called through the same words and the door latch clicked and her shadow disappeared up the close. They would have turned in before she got back, whenever that would be.

She knew the inside of that caravan too well. She became

intimate with its every detail. There was the bed, which dou-
bled as a table and bench seats, framed on three sides by
brown-and-yellow curtains that were never open. The sleeping bag was shiny purple on the outside and sky-blue cotton
on the inside. The kettle and portable were both gone. His
hi-vis singlet dangled from a wardrobe door. There was a gas
hob with two rusty rings and a cylinder under it, a biscuit tin
with stale crumbs and dust. There was a bank calendar that
was three years out of date, with a photo of a different fading
landscape for every month. It never budged off June, even
when July was well under way. It was always strand and
ocean in the distance, a foreground of harebells and heather.

The light grew grey between four and five. She knew
that it grew light between four and five because she wasn't
always asleep then. Sometimes she was conscious, seasick.
Sometimes she lay alone, watching light grey gradually filling the horizon, the close, the caravan. Where had Marcus
gone? She could still feel the bulk of him on top of her, the
thick blunt spike of him coring up into her. Where did everyone go?

She tiptoed up to the same townhouse. From the
entrance she spoke Marcus's name into the interior black.
No answer. She moved forward, stepping the way she had
that one time when he had held both her hands and drawn
her into him. She closed her eyes. It was just like her wedding day. She remembered closing her eyes for a moment
after Paul, who had given her away, took one of her hands
and asked her if she was ready. She surprised herself with the
memory. Her sister had remembered everything for both of
them. All the faces in the rows of seats on either side of
the aisle, all turning towards them when the organ started

bellowing in the choir balcony, and all the flowers up there at the altar gates. How did the girl, who was only a baby then, know what Helen's dress had been like?

When she opened her eyes again, there was a speck on the floor of the downstairs room of the townhouse. It was a tiny orange glow at first, like a planet light years out in space. The ball! It was the plastic golf ball that Marcus had brought and she, with him pressed hard behind her, had chipped through the window's black hole. It was the orange ball they had forgotten all about, and it was luminous.

She stood gazing at it for the longest time. The more she stood gazing at the ball, the huger its glow became. It drew all available light into itself and burned it like fuel. She could almost smell her skin burning, the singeing of her hair. You would never have imagined that there could be any light in there to draw upon, but there must have been. There must have been zillions of sparks and scintillas and rays and glimmers swimming around and yet so infinitesimal as to be invisible to her naked eye. Now they were being sucked into the magnetic field that the ball appeared to radiate. Now they were burning, being renewed and being burned again.

4

THE NEWS WAS not good. Paul asked how long, as if he were looking at lit X-rays in a consultant's office. End of the week. The staff was skeletal. The operation was being moved to the East. Far or Near? Who knew? The guy even suggested that Paul would have been let go long before now, but for his circumstances.

'My circumstances.'

'You know.'

Paul shook his hand, left the building and ran to where his bike was locked, got honked at twice on the ring road, cutting across lanes, breaking lights. His daughter was standing out on the close's dust track in her pyjamas. 'I felt safer outside,' she said.

'What the hell is going on?'

'She's not in her room.'

Paul let his bike go, and heard it hit the ground behind him. Up the stairs: Martina's humid room, his own, the girl's. He was shocked to find nothing; more than anything he was shocked to realize, once again, how disappointed he was to find nothing. There was no answer from the caravan. He picked up his bike from where he had dropped it and coaxed his daughter back inside, insisting that Martina would be back.

'Simple reason?'

'There is,' he said. 'There has to be.'

He told her about the job. He said that he was delighted. To prove it, he burned his suit in one of the empty oil drums on the site. They sprawled out the back, splitting Martina's last small bottle of rosé from the fridge, as ribbons of black smoke from Paul's burning suit tangled upwards into the clear sky, and not once mentioning that there was still no sign of Martina. They slept in, were fairly silent over lunch and walked the mile and a bit that it took to reach the centre of the town from their close. It was mid-afternoon and they felt like aliens. It was, Paul said, like a coach tour of the Balkans, where you take a pit-stop in one of those dying hamlets that had been the centre of some medieval empire. A few upright chairs outside open terrace doors, bearing magazines so out of date they must be used as fans. A handful of lurchers sniffing around the base of a granite statue. A stack of bikes unlocked at the top of the street. The hum of a wireless through someone's open window.

The shops were desolate. Even the minimart, usually stocked with tat for passing traffic, felt empty. Paul bought a net of satsumas and a Sharpie of royal washable blue for the girl, but there was nobody to pay. He tapped a coin's rim against the checkout, called through the 'Staff Only' door and, when nobody answered or came through, poured a fistful of spare change onto the rubber belt without bothering to count it. There was footpath for half a mile of road from the edge of town, and none for the second half-mile after the supermarket. They stepped into long grass and briars whenever they heard a car coming. Twice they made way, and twice nothing came.

He waited until almost eleven, when it was starting to get

properly dark and there was a light clearly glowing from the caravan.

'I'm going up to ask Marcus.'

'I'm coming.'

'Stay where you are. Me and Marcus need to have a proper chat.'

He made that last bit sound like there would be raised voices, language. She was better off sitting tight. When there was still no answer from the caravan, he tried the locked handle. No Marcus. Not much of anything, except for some class of bed, visible through a gap in the curtains, where Marcus must have got his head down. With the light off his bike, he went into the townhouse nearest the caravan.

'Marcus?'

His voice sounded thin, hollow, in the black cavities that were intended to be rooms. He thought he could hear footsteps. He started whistling. Had he ever whistled before? He couldn't remember ever whistling. Yet there he was, trying to hold still a light that was dwindling fast, edging through the shell of a half-built apartment block, and whistling for all he was worth to keep himself company. All the floor's crap had been swept into a single pile in one of the rooms: broken pallets, buckled screws, scraps of piping, foam pellets and dust. At the centre, what must have been the entrance hall, a wooden ladder leaned up into a fathomless rectangle.

'Hello?' Flood answered on the ninth ring, just as Paul was preparing to speak to the recorded message.

'Flood?'

This was the following day. Paul had promised his daughter, when he came down from the site, that he would try Flood. She had written out what to say while Paul watched her. She was still in her pyjamas. Her hair was pure black, just like her mother's. The hand holding her Sharpie had little patches of eczema around the knuckles. Though twelve and getting lanky, she had looked small and vulnerable with her clipped accent and her series of bullet-points. Paul hadn't wanted to call Flood, in case Flood pressed about rent that was owing, but the girl insisted.

When he answered, Flood sounded as if he was waiting to hear from someone else.

'Yes?'

'It's Paul. From number seven?'

'Yes?'

It wasn't clear whether or not Flood had any idea who Paul was. It was weeks since he had called in. Apart from that first visit, he and Paul had hardly exchanged two words. Paul needed to speak quickly, before Flood hung up.

'I need to speak with Marcus.'

'Okay . . .' The Flood of a few months before had been so sure of himself, with all the time in the world, shooting the breeze with the ladies, full of lame flirts and riddles. This Flood had a way of sounding cornered, one that seemed to dread what Paul might ask of him. 'What can I do for you?'

'I just need to talk to Marcus.' Paul didn't want to say about Martina going missing, and he reckoned Flood knew nothing about her and his nephew. 'Just some stuff on site.'

'Okay. I'll pass on the message.'

'Can you not give me his number?' It sounded as if the line had gone dead. 'Hello?'

'Hello.'

'Can you not give me Marcus's number?'

'No.'

'No?'

'No.'

'No, as in you won't give me Marcus's mobile number?'

'Can't.' The far end of the line rustled. 'Can't, won't, same difference.'

'I'll go up myself and see him tonight so.'

It was then, only then, that Flood cleared his throat and spoke something resembling the truth. 'He won't be there tonight,' Flood said. 'He won't be there tomorrow night either. He hasn't been on site since the end of last month.'

'Excuse me?' Paul knew he shouldn't have come across as stunned as he did, but he couldn't help himself. 'His light is on in the caravan every night. I've seen him around too.'

'The light in the caravan's been on a timer for the past three weeks. Maybe you saw his shadow, but it wasn't Marcus. There wasn't funds to keep Marcus on site. He was offered a start in Reading and he took it.'

'So who's been looking after the place?'

Instead of answering that, Flood rattled on awhile about times being bad and not getting better any time soon. All these weeks, had Martina been dolling herself up to visit an empty caravan? It was as if, Flood was wittering, they were back where they'd started and the whole shebang never happened: places closing all around you and no life anywhere.

'Are we nearer completion your end?'

'Completion?' Paul had no idea what Flood was on about. 'I wish.'

'That family from the midlands might be moving in. Any day now.'

Flood had promised the same thing two months ago. There was no family from the midlands. The family from the midlands was a mirage, a dim collective ruse shimmering out there on the horizon.

'Fantastic,' Paul said finally. 'Us and all the other neighbours will be sure to throw them a huge fucking beach party when they land.'

'Then where did she go?' The girl was sitting on one of the chairs at the picnic table. Paul didn't tell her that Marcus wasn't around, only that Flood knew nothing. Even as she asked that, her voice seemed to be breaking. 'We saw her go up. Remember?'

The girl cried. She was probably crying for Martina and her mother all at once. Mostly, she had seemed a bit dazed for months. But the shock had been short-circuited for his daughter as well, Paul could see, by Martina's being there, being so like Helen and so prepared to think the best. Now Martina was gone as well. Now the forty-eight hours which the officers had said see most similar cases resolved were almost up. Paul went around to his daughter's side of the kitchen table and held her small face against his T-shirt's logo.

'It's okay,' he kept repeating. 'It's okay.'

'So be it.'

They said nothing about this either, just as they had said nothing to one another about Helen. They said nothing about Martina's absence, her possible whereabouts. Paul withheld the fact that Martina had been pretending to wander up the close to pay visits to someone who had weeks since left the country. Had she, after a fashion, followed

Marcus to Reading? That didn't sound like the kind of thing Martina would do, any more than Helen. And what if she had done? Good luck to her, Paul thought. His daughter said nothing to Paul about the words on the kitchen window that she and Martina had found, washed away, and couldn't help chirping at every opportunity since. Paul said nothing to her, yet, about what he had seen up in the townhouses. Nor did he make any reference to the way in which his daughter had moved into her auntie's room, was sleeping in her unlaundered bedclothes and had taken to wearing her ochre lip-gloss.

In fact, they said nothing about Martina to anybody. There was really nobody to say anything to. Martina and Helen had been one another's only family. Paul didn't report Martina's absence to the authorities, nor did he decide not to. He just never got around to making a phone call. When his daughter asked him if he was going to, he said he was afraid of how it would make them look to the outside world. He said he was afraid she would be taken from him.

Slattery started putting in appearances. They knew it was him, even before they spoke to him. He had the very demeanour Flood had described – of one who forgot that he no longer owned that plot, making free with all the unoc-cupied houses and their flotsam. He came down the hill between the row opposite and the townhouses, across the green area that still had no grass seeded on it. One day he just seemed to fade into view out of scrub and bushes. After that, he came down so frequently that there were tracks from the tyres of his quad in the long grass on the hill up to his place.

He looked in his late fifties at least – a small man, though it was hard to tell since he never climbed down off the quad; as if coming in contact with this earth would wither him in an instant. He wore a tweed fedora and one of those quilted sleeveless horsey gilets in navy blue. The girl even referred to his quad as his horse. She spent her afternoons at the window of the master bedroom, surveying the close. She kept Martina's penniless phone charged and with her, in case of any calls or texts.

'Here he comes!' she would shout down through the silent house. Or 'Your friend is coming on his horse.'

Slattery had nothing in particular to do. He was just snooping. He appeared at the same hour most evenings, after the spite had gone out of the sun and before it had started its slow descent, cruising from shell to shell in low gear. Sometimes he would come to a standstill, raise himself slightly off his saddle and peer into each abyss. Sometimes you could see him shake his head before inching forward again. He came up their side of the close once.

'He's coming our way!'

Slattery paused right outside the front window of Sheila's empty place. Paul had gone upstairs to watch as well. Slattery was having a proper gawk in through the bay window of number three. He shook his chubby head again, reversed back out into the dust and disappeared into the rear access between number three and number four. He was out of sight so long that they thought he must have gone home and they had somehow missed his going. Next thing, he was at the end of their drive. He was braking.

'Can I help you?'

Paul had run downstairs and stepped nonchalantly out

onto their doormat. In Marcus's absence, Paul had appointed himself unofficial site watchman. Not that there was much to watch over. It was just something to do, a distraction from the aimlessness of their days.

'I beg your pardon.'

Slattery was hamming up surprise when he said that. He was pretending he had no idea that anyone lived there. He pronounced 'pardon' as if he had a hard-boiled egg lodged on his tongue and the word rhymed with 'Gordon'. Was Slattery's first name Gordon? He certainly looked like a Gordon, to Paul standing there unshaven and thick with the tedium of another stifling evening.

'I suppose,' Slattery said, 'this makes you and me neighbours.' He pointed backwards up the hill, in the direction of the horse-chestnuts. He smiled a smile of benevolence. He was, after all, treating Paul as an equal of sorts. 'Howdy, neighbour.'

Slattery was assuming that Paul knew all about him. Paul knew all about him, but really did not want to give Slattery the satisfaction. Paul sauntered down the drive, taking one hand from a pocket of his shorts.

'I suppose it does,' he said. Slattery's hand, when they shook, was cold and damp. It was also strangely small. It wasn't like the hand of a grown man. It was slender, weak and weightless. 'Paul.'

'That's right,' Slattery said. 'Paul.'

'I didn't quite catch—'

'No, no,' Slattery said. 'We know all about you, Paul.' He removed the fedora. He had arrived with the air of one whose words came preformed, had been tested many times in their own echoes and proven to be sufficiently appropriate. 'You have our sympathies, Paul.'

Two minutes before, Slattery had been doing his little shock routine. Now here he was, not only admitting that he'd known they were there, but admitting, too, that he had read all about them in the papers. Or, rather, some anonymous plural (in which Slattery included himself) had known and had read all about them.

'Who's "we"?'

'Forgive me.' Slattery replaced his fedora, back to business, a tad put out by Paul's bluntness. 'Myself and Hazel.'

Nobody was entirely sure where Slattery made his money. That was what Flood had told Helen. The one consensus seemed to be that nobody with a name like Slattery could be to the manor born. Dog food, some said. A handful of factories around the country. There was talk, too, that he had married into a dog-food fortune and had acquired the nobility of dog food overnight.

'Haze is a big fan.'

'Haze?'

'The little lady.' For a second there, Slattery looked unsure if Paul and he spoke the same language. 'Hazel.' He squinted. He seemed to reach the decision, right in front of Paul, to speak slowly to him. 'I call her Haze. She's a huge fan. Of yours.'

'Of mine?' Paul wondered if Slattery was making fun of him. 'Aren't they all?'

'I beg your pardon.' There it went again, the hard-boiled egg. 'I phrased it tactlessly. Forgive me.' It was becoming obvious that Slattery had an errand to run, that he was not trucking further distraction, that Paul was the errand. 'My little lady has admired how you have disported yourself through this whole . . .' he threw one hand away from himself, seeking the precise word '. . . trauma?' Was 'trauma' the precise word? Had Helen been beaten to a pulp and found naked from the waist down in some shore-bound field up the coast, gnawed to the bone by crows and stoats? Was that the truth Paul had deleted from his hard drive? Slattery looked so positive that 'trauma' was the precise word. 'Haze has all the cuttings and she talks about you all the time. She has asked me to tell you that if ever there is anything we can do for you, not to hesitate.'

Slattery did something with the right handle of his quad. It locked into reverse and twisted backwards, away from Paul.

'Anything at all,' Slattery was calling from the dust pluming around him. What did Slattery have in mind? Babysitting? A spot of landscaping? 'Anything.'

'What was all that about?' the girl asked, when her father came back into the house. She had been watching from upstairs. The last thing she needed, Paul figured, was Slattery's little lady's obsession with their 'trauma'.

'Who knows?' Paul said. 'A prick.'

Slattery came back about an hour later. It was just starting to get dark. He didn't knock or anything of the sort. He simply braked at the end of their drive once again and flashed the headlamps of his quad. Paul and the girl were sitting at the flicker of their flat screen. The room lit and blackened and lit again in a few short jabs, like sheet lightning minus thunder.

'Come for supper.' The voice still belonged to Slattery, but the person was scarcely visible behind the beam of the quad. Just the outline of the fedora. 'Haze insists.'

'You're very good.'

Paul had come back to the front step. He had his top off, was in the shorts he wore cycling and in bed. He was shielding his eyes with his left hand. He was speaking down to the beam, through the engine's grumble, to the disembodied voice behind it. Supper chez Slattery sounded like a night in hell. Slattery may well have been the prick everybody said he was, but he was still the only prick kind enough to invite them over.

'Shall we say the Friday of next week? Sevenish?'

'Perfect.'

'Not this Friday. We have to go away. The following Friday, next week.' He was determined to be understood, Slattery was, amid the noise and the glare. 'Not this one coming. The next one.'

Paul's eyes were aching. 'You're very good.'

Two men moved into Sheila's empty house. They worked in construction, judging by the cut of them: jeans and boots spattered with chalk and paint. They looked, indeed, like brothers. They were gone all day every day, weekends included, in an old station-wagon with strange plates, which they parked at odd angles to Flood's barrier, ferrying all manner of gear to and from the house. Their patio door was open every evening, through which wafted loud trashy rock and the smells of frying meats. Paul referred to them as 'the Poles', though they could have been from anywhere. They certainly didn't appear to have a word of English, and they never waved or acknowledged the presence of their neighbours.

'I'm Paul.'

Paul had rung their doorbell and the one who answered

looked askance at him and then said, 'No, thank you,' like those words were his only learned phrase and served as an answer to everything. Maybe he thought Paul was selling chattels door-to-door.

'No.' Paul laughed. He waved up the close. 'I live there. In number seven.' Then he pointed at himself, deliberately. 'Paul.' He held out his hand to be shaken.

The Pole just looked at it, confused, and said again, 'No, thank you,' stiltedly, before closing the door. Paul stood there almost a minute, considering knocking again, laughing some more and shaking his head. All the curtains had been removed. Sheila's furniture was stacked in the front room. Through the double doors to the kitchen there were units and a row of sleeping bags on the tiled floor.

The sun kept beating. The sun kept beating until the whole world, it felt, was dried to parchment. The back garden remained clumps of topsoil, with only scraps of limp weeds here and there. Martina's creepers had not thrived. A slip came through the letterbox with a notice warning about the danger of fires started carelessly. It lay there for days among flyers for takeaways and bank letters with red print on them. What fires there were, they thought, were way off in the distance and seemed confined to gorse. Then Marcus's caravan burned to the ground. It must have been in the small hours. It must have blazed hard, but they heard and saw nothing. One morning it was walls melted inwards, innards still smoking.

A different night, Paul was woken by the sound of water splashing downstairs. At first he assumed that it was some sort of wish-fulfilling dream and just lay where he was. When it kept running, he went down and found the cold tap in the kitchen sink on full blast. They must have left it on by accident. He sat up the next night, the cold tap on, and the same thing happened. Three to five o'clock. The flow got strong and the water properly cold. Paul figured that the mains back on at night was a secret few enough knew about. They set alarms, sleepwalked down to the sink and filled their bottles. Some nights they were more awake, and sat up tippling from Martina's plastic picnic glasses as if tap water were Prosecco. They felt merry and full of hope, while yet another glaring dawn grew gradually across the back wall.

The girl found fortune cookies from the Chinese take-away Martina had bought. They were in a drawer. Each was still in its cellophane, tasted of nothing but sugar and had a little rectangle of paper in its hollow centre.

'*Soon life will become more interesting,*' the girl read.

'*Don't look down upon yourself,*' Paul read.

'*In the end all things will be known.*'

'*You are a person of another time.*'

The Poles seemed to multiply and disappear at will. You never saw the same head twice. Neither of the original brothers, as Paul called them, was anywhere in sight. There were times he thought there was nobody in number three, nor ever had been. Other evenings there would be three jalopies lined up outside, or you would glimpse half a dozen of them, all men, walking in a pack on the hard shoulder of the ring road with bottles of water bought in the same discount supermarket where Martina had got the sun-loungers.

Then it was August. The mains had dried up altogether. Like the Poles, Paul and the girl were surviving on bought bottles. They would walk to the discount supermarket and wheel a trolley full of translucent litres packed in cubes back along the road and just leave each trolley to die a slow death up on the site. They drank from bottles, made tea with it, rationed what they drank. The attic tank was dry. Its pipes, without any current flowing through them, made occasional whale music. They filled a basin in the bathroom every morning, and took turns to wash in that. The girl went first, since washing in his daughter's water didn't bother Paul. Last thing every night, they used the day's basin to flush the toilet, which was filled with scraps of roll.

There was comfort in the noise the Poles made. They could be heard most nights in the garden of number three, talking loudly, laughing. It always sounded like they were drinking, but jolly with it. The racket made Paul feel safer and the slight murk of the evenings more approachable. For a while, he and his daughter even started sitting out the back again, watching the sun set somewhere over the wall and the hedgerows beyond.

'What's the chances of them feeding us dog food?'

'Stop,' Paul said.

They were at Slattery's door when she said that about the dog food. They had taken the shortcut up through the slope of high grass. They considered going the long way round, turning right out the road, trekking the hundred yards or so, then turning right again when they came to the entrance to Slattery's avenue. But it was far too hot for such formalities. They had cut through the undergrowth, skirted the mountain of rocks and muck, and walked in the tracks Slattery had flattened with his quad. She had walked up one track, Paul the other. After two-thirds of the distance, the long grass became lawn, staked saplings and gravel. The tracks

Slattery's quad had ground went around to the rear to what looked like stables. A sign said, 'Goose eggs for sale'. Peonies spilled out of decommissioned cannon shells.

'Guys!'

They had heard hounds yelping and Slattery whistling. When Slattery dragged the door towards himself, half a dozen things chimed and rattled. He hadn't struck Paul as a 'guys' kind of guy, but you never can tell. Slattery looked them up and down. He had made it sound informal when they'd spoken. So informal that Paul and the girl hadn't even bothered to change before leaving.

'Just the pair of you,' he said. 'We were expecting herself as well.' When Slattery had referenced their trauma so delicately, Paul assumed that he knew all about Helen's disappearance. Slattery pointed at the stubble Paul had let grow into a proper beard. 'Love the whiskers.'

The front door must have been seldom used. They had to wade through walking sticks, shotguns and golf umbrellas. Slattery parked them in a room with a white carpet and the smell of something rotting.

'Darling!' Slattery was yodelling into his hallway's vaulted silence. 'Haze?'

When Hazel neither appeared nor answered, he said, retreating from the room, 'She's very excited about your coming, perhaps even a little nervous.'

Paul made a face at his daughter in the three-seater that backed onto the centre of the room. Behind the sofa there was a table with an antique rotary-dial phone that looked carved from ivory. They weren't as flush as Slattery would have you think. The upholstery was threadbare at the edges and had wisps of horsehair hanging out of it. The carpet was stained and worn thin. The girl whispered that the sofa felt damp. She moved onto a leather ottoman that had several substantial gashes in it. The coffee-table was a battered trunk covered with glossy dog magazines that had mug rings on them. Paul held up one of the magazines and mouthed, 'Dogs!'

The air felt damp, which probably accounted for the fire being lit with slabs of rough turf. When Slattery returned alone, bearing a silver salver of drinks already poured, Paul was standing inspecting the over-mantel.

'Gilt,' Slattery said.

'What?'

'The frame. It's gilt.' They both grinned at the misunder-standing, Slattery more so than Paul. 'Gilt without the U in it. The best sort.'

'Very good.'

With every chuckle, Slattery shook. Paul watched him shaking, the velvet of his jacket, the ripples of burgundy cor-duroy and the quivers of flesh visible beneath. His skin looked fresher, more youthful, than Paul had remembered. Brow all perspiration beads, Slattery handed drinks around.

'Please.'

Tonic mostly, two lemon wedges and dry gin measured out by the thimbleful. The girl as well. It seemed to be the only option. Slattery flopped into the long sofa and Paul tried to ignore his host's feet not quite reaching the white carpet.

'Sad news.' Slattery nodded backwards through the long windows down the hill. He didn't look all that sad. 'About our friend Flood.'

'I haven't actually heard.'

'How have you not?' Slattery looked delighted to be the bearer of the news. 'Front-page stuff. On the run. Creditors galore, all wondering where on earth Signor Flood has scarpered off to.'

Paul felt stung on Flood's behalf. He wanted to say that Flood's disgrace explained Slattery's recent presence on the manor, but there were hours yet to grin through and Flood hardly deserved Paul's loyalty. Instead, he stirred his drink with his little finger.

'Forgive me! Were you pals?' Slattery slid to the edge of the sofa until his feet were just about grazing the carpet.

'Me and Flood?' Paul's daughter was staring at him. She looked unsure of what her father would say. 'Eh, no . . .'

'Portgal.' Slattery missed the middle vowel both times he said that. 'Apparently our friend has been sighted in Portgal.'

'Which has no U in it either,' Paul said. 'Apparently.'

'Pardon me?'

Hazel was unexpected. She came out of nowhere, with so little ceremony that she was in the middle of the room before anyone noticed her entrance.

'Ah, Haze,' Slattery shouted. Was she deaf? 'Good girl. Now's the chance to meet your hero.'

Paul had pictured some fusty dame in twin-set and gardening gloves. The real Hazel was half Slattery's age. That, or Slattery wasn't as old as he initially seemed. What was the phrase he had used? 'The little lady' . . . She was poured into a class of flamenco combination: black ribbed dress and thick heels. She had a white perm gelled back at the temples, heavy black mascara and, odder still, satin elbow gloves that were snipped coarsely at the fingers to reveal nails polished black as well. She said nothing. Even when Paul said, 'Thank you for having us,' Hazel said nothing.

'How are we looking?' Hazel did something Slattery took as assent. 'Good girl. Smells delicious.'

She led them through to an open-plan modern kitchen littered with dog bowls. Was she mute as well as deaf? They could have been forgiven for thinking their hostess was mute. She had uttered zilch so far. She had barely acknowledged them. Not until she turned from the oven towards them, with a flat casserole dish cupped in silicon pads, did she finally move her lips. 'Paul.' Her voice had a tremble in it. So did her hand.

Slattery stood, wielding a serving spoon, and ladled onto their plates hefty portions of meat and dumpling and pearl onion all bound in thick brown gloop. 'Can't go wrong with goulash,' he said. 'Please tell me there are no veggies among us.'

'No.'

The look on the girl's face said what had occurred to Paul too late, namely that one or both of them could have excused themselves from the main course on ideological grounds.

'No,' Paul said. 'Both carnivores.'

'Paul.'

Twice Hazel had spoken now, and each time she had mumbled the same name. Paul glanced first at Slattery, then at the girl, searching for some clue of what was expected of him.

'Forgive me,' Slattery said. 'Drinks.'

Slattery placed a pitcher of iced water at the centre of the dining-table and disappeared into a different room on the other side of the kitchen. They could hear bottles chink, their host chuntering to himself. The ice was melting quickly in the pitcher, almost visibly, at the surface of the water. When it was first put down, Paul could see his daughter through it, distorted by the pitcher's curves. Then condensation was forming on the outside of its glass, making it opaque and his daughter less visible. It was thickening. It was gathering into drips that streamed down and made a wet ring on the tablecloth. For months the inside of Paul's mouth, its roof, tongue and throat, had scraped like sandpaper. Without thinking, Paul reached forward and caught a falling drip with the end of one finger before the drip hit the bottom, and he sucked it. It was so beautifully cold.

'Do help yourself.' Slattery had a bottle of red in one paw, a corkscrew in the other. His face was pure puzzlement. 'By all means.'

'Paul.'

Was Hazel's speech confined to one syllable? Slattery poured wine into goblets that had stems stained blue, insisting that their guests tuck in while the food was still hot.

Talk was of Flood. The cowboy Flood was. 'Cowboy' was the word Slattery kept using. Paul caught his daughter's eye. The girl had yet to touch her food. She hadn't even handled her cutlery. She was staring at her plate. Paul took a lump of bread from the middle of the table and swabbed it with sauce. It tasted of nothing except salt and grease.

'Are we all grand?'

It was Hazel who said that. Seated now, she had spoken once again. She scarcely moved her lips when she spoke. Her voice was feathery, begging extra attention.

'Grand,' Paul said. 'Just waiting for it to cool.'

Flood was one of a thousand similar cowboys, all coming over the hill on their horses. While Slattery spoke, Hazel concentrated on eating as delicately as she could. Her nerves, of which Slattery had warned them, seemed real. Apart from Slattery's bark, the loudest thing in the room was Hazel's knife and fork trying not to clink on the china of her plate. There was something touching about her. Notwithstanding Slattery's bluster, having Paul and his daughter to dinner did appear to be a big deal. She had gone to far too much trouble, with her appearance and with the place-settings: napkins folded into swans. There was something vacant about her as well, Paul thought. Was she all there?

Alas, Slattery was saying, the cowboys had taken over, the cowboys had *carte blanche*.

'The cowboys?'

'Flood and his ilk.'

'Of course.' Paul had a piece of gristle in his cheek. He was waiting for a distraction to spit it into his napkin, trying not to gag. 'It's really delicious.'

'Shall I tell them what I call the development, honey?'

'Paul.'

'I call it Flanders . . . You know. All the muck and shrapnel. All the poppies, one for every dismembered body lying decomposed underneath. One for every skeleton.'

'Paul.'

'Very good.'

'I call it Flanders Fields. I wander down at sunset some evenings, as you know, and I always holler the same thing leaving, don't I, honey? *I'm off to Flanders Fields*, I always holler.'

'Yeah.' Paul was getting freaked by Hazel's repeated chirping of his name. He was put out, as well, by his host's description of what was still their home. 'Very witty.'

War was Slattery's thing. He had dozens of glossy coffee-table tomes on it. He had compiled an inventory of names from the surrounding parishes of young chaps – the sons of good families and farm labourers alike – who had all signed up together in the local post office and had perished together within weeks.

'Paul.'

'All right, Haze, all right.'

Slattery stood again, though mostly it was hard to tell, and poured more wine for everyone, except the girl, who had scarcely touched hers. She was too busy sliding lumps around her plate and occasionally lifting a fork with a morsel on it to her lips. After draining the bottle, Slattery left the room.

Paul pleaded with his daughter to eat properly. He didn't really give a damn. He was just trying to fill the air deadened by Slattery's absence.

'Please,' Paul said to her, 'don't let me down.'

'Eat what you like, sweetie.' The more puce with wine the inside of Hazel's mouth got, the more her tongue loosened. 'Ignore your daddy.'

In spite of the amnesty, or maybe because of it, the girl shovelled several large forkfuls into her mouth and followed them each with a hefty slug of wine. They sat watching her until Slattery returned with a couple of pieces of memorabilia that he had bought at auction: a pair of scissors prised from dead enemy hands; a gas mask the colour of copper. He gave the scissors to the girl: crooked, rusting at the handle, bearing a Gothic inscription on the inside of one of its blades that the girl read aloud, her mouth half full.

'*Kettenhunde.*'

'Very impressive,' Slattery said. 'And its meaning?'

'Chained dogs,' the girl said.

Slattery was adamant that Paul should try on the gas mask. He stood behind Paul and forced the straps at the back. The inside smelt of old rubber and of sick. Paul raised his glass of wine and, for a joke, tried to take a drink. While the others laughed, Paul swallowed the piece of gristle he had been holding in his cheek all that time and felt his throat coated in its grease. He could hear, but he could hardly see a thing and he couldn't push off the gas mask. Slattery was jabbering on, explaining to 'the ladies' that he had spent a weekend with it on once, that wearing it gave you a bird's-eye view of what it was like to be actually in a war and facing the enemy. Who was the enemy?

Paul tried to remove the gas mask, but the thing felt suctioned to his head. He tried to say, 'Please help me get it off,' but he could hear how muffled his voice was by all the tubing, and the others only laughed again.

'If you say so,' Slattery said.

'Paul.'

The mask's goggles got fogged with his breathing. The straps at the back of his head had no give in them. The other three were receding into mist: Slattery prattling on about craftsmanship, only the girl's expression and Hazel's voice displaying any awareness of what was happening.

'Paul.'

Paul stood, tugging at the straps and growling, 'Please get the fucking thing off me.' Slattery came behind him and said to take slow, even breaths. When they finally yanked off the mask, Paul's beard was dripping sweat, his hair everywhere, and they were staring at him as they might a scuba diver dragged up after a sudden loss of pressure.

'Cheese and coffee?'

Hazel fetched a hand towel for Paul to rub his head down. It smelt of petrol, the towel did. She said, 'I wish Martina could have made it.'

'Martina?' Paul didn't dare look at his daughter. Slattery must have meant Martina when he said that, out on the doorstep, about a third person. 'Made what?'

'Here. Tonight,' Hazel said. 'I wish Martina could have made it here tonight.'

'I said that, honey.' Slattery was balancing cheeses on a marble block. 'When they arrived, I said we had been expecting all three of them.'

'Isn't Martina your wife's sister?'

'I warned you she was a huge fan.' Slattery was blushing. Or was that just the wine and the heat of the kitchen and the summer that was in it? 'Fetch your scrapbook, Haze.'

The scrapbook was wrapped in floral-embossed wallpaper, and in it was glued every cutting they knew about from all the newspapers. Hazel had even taken a poster from one of the filling stations out the road and folded it in two. She held the scrapbook longest at the article that featured a photo of them all: Paul, his daughter, Martina, seated on the sill of the bay window. The reflection of the flash in the double-glazing had made a blind spot of Martina's head. Hazel was rubbing her thumb around and around the bright sun where Martina's face should have been.

'Has she gone out?'

'Martina?'

'Has she a hot date?' Hazel asked.

'Kind of thing.'

'You know I met them?' Slattery said.

'Really?' Paul wasn't sure how much he could trust Slattery's word. 'Both of them?'

'Your wife mainly. I saw them together in Rainey's around the end of May.'

'In?'

'Rainey's?' Slattery sounded suspicious of Paul's igno-rance. 'The supermarket and lounge just down the road. It belongs to the Rainey family.'

'News to me.'

'I bumped into them there at the end of May and bought them drinks. I spoke to your wife only, to be honest, not to her sister.'

Helen and Martina did go to the pictures together, once, and did stop for one at the lounge belonging to the supermarket.

'She mentioned something all right.'

'Perhaps they had no idea who I was.' When Paul didn't protest, Slattery gave a petty shrug. 'I told your wife I had known their folks.'

'Did you?'

'Oh, yes. Not well, obviously, but I had met both of them at different times.'

That wasn't what Paul meant. He wasn't asking Slattery if he had really known their parents. He was asking if Slattery had said that to Helen. Paul had never known anyone raise their parents with Helen or Martina.

This was why they had been invited. It had to be. Slattery

had a smile that said, 'In your own time . . .' All those years of skirting around Helen's past, of accepting Martina's presence and her protectiveness of her sister, of keeping the girl in the dark. Nobody had ever asked Paul anything. Even Helen had scarcely spoken of it. Oddly, this moment, at the table of a stranger whose wealth was rumoured to come from food manufactured for consumption by dogs, was the closest Paul had ever got to its core. It is conceivable that he wanted to say something, to spill whatever was left to him, but there was still his daughter to think of. His shoulders ached: he was only propping the floodgates shut a while longer.

How much did Slattery know? More than him? There were times Paul wondered if parts of the truth, and therefore its entirety, had been withheld from him. Slattery wanted juice. You could all but hear the saliva accumulating in his jowls. He could swing for it, Slattery could. Slattery could swing for whatever dirt he was chasing. They all could. Refusing to meet their fat faces gazing at him, Paul pushed his plate towards the centre of the table and coughed.

Slattery finally said, 'Unimaginable, really.'

The girl vomited onto her plate. Just like that. She had eaten every scrap, had sat in pale speechlessness, and now was heaving loudly all over her place-setting shreds of animal flesh swimming in acrid human stomach acid.

'Something didn't agree with you,' Slattery said.

Paul hauled her to the sink. With the second substantial heave came stuff other than food or bile. There was dust in there, sawdust. There were also tiny shards of wood, masonry and steel. Paul tried to run the taps to wash it away before anyone else saw, but nothing came out.

'We should leave.'

'A quick coffee?'

'She's covered in sick.' Was Slattery, Paul's tone meant to ask, even thicker than he appeared? 'I should really get her home.'

At the door, Slattery said something about going to 'Portgal' until the end of the summer, about hooking up when they got back. The door dragged shut behind them, the crunch of gravel underfoot ceased and the long grass was silver in the light of a torch borrowed from their hosts.

'It looks strange from up here,' the girl said.

They could see the outline of the close, their house alarm's blue strobe, and the town's and ring road's smattering of lights in the distance.

'Freaks!' Paul screamed into the darkness. The air was too dry for echoes.

The girl laughed and screamed too. 'Bloody freaks!'

The Poles were at it full throttle. A bigger than usual gang, a ghetto-blaster cranked up, some drunken singing, raised voices and possibly even a scuffle. By two a.m., Paul had had enough. He pulled on his tracksuit bottoms and thumped on their bell. Nothing. The rear gate was locked. He climbed onto one of their bins and, when there was no evidence of a party, jumped into their garden. Though the patio light was still on, the kitchen was unlit and empty. He could see yellow coming down the stairs, and there seemed to be movement up there. He shielded his eyes and, pressing against the back door, glimpsed only himself in what must have been a long mirror against the nearest wall. His two images, on the glass and on the mirror behind it, were like concentric reflections.

They receded when he stepped backwards. When he moved closer again, they loomed into one another, frame into frame, gaze into gaze, mouth into hollow mouth.

'Jesus Christ!'

'What happened?'

There was no hiding it, not now or any more, to his bleary-eyed daughter standing in slippers in their hall, dead-lock bolted behind him.

'There was nobody there for anything to happen,' he said. 'Nobody except some nutter staring straight back out at me.'

After the water, the money ran out. The phone line went dead, and with it the modem. Even the electricity stopped pumping into their walls. A couple of times a week they walked to the library, where she charged her laptop for free at a power point beneath the back shelves and he riffled the local papers trying to find some mention of Flood's fall from grace. Nobody said anything to them. Otherwise, they made do with Helen's scented candles scattered from the bathroom throughout the house, and with Slattery's torch, used sparingly to save on batteries. The banging on their door resumed, sometimes in the small hours, sometimes during the day. The envelopes piled inside the letterbox. One day a page with red writing was glued to the door.

'What does it say?'

'Something about repossession,' he said. 'Nothing to do with us.'

They started sleeping in the attic, to get as far away from the banging as they could. Paul laid a few unscrewed wardrobe doors as flooring and squeezed two mattresses up through the trap into the attic. It was sweltering up there, with no window and all that hot air under the roof and the smell of melting wax. Mostly he read paperbacks that had been stacked on Martina's bedside stool, while his daughter kept trying to video-call old schoolfriends via a weak unencrypted signal she occasionally picked up. Paul had saved the last satsuma from the bag he had bought in the supermarket. He held it over a flame and gazed at it, marvelling at its glow. He gazed at it so long that its zest began singeing. The girl's calls kept dropping or, worse, being scrambled by a high-pitched whistle or a monotonous backbeat. One by one, the disembodied voices receded. It was too much, lying there, eyes shut, hearing your daughter asking, *'Kannst du mich hören?'* or *'Hallo, ist da jemand?'* of a mute screen.

'They can't hear you,' he said. 'There's nobody there, pet.'

Once, no sleep to be had up in that furnace, he asked from one side of the darkness to the other, 'Why did she keep saying my name?'

'Who?'

'Haze. Frau Slattery.' He could hear his daughter sniggering gently. 'All she kept saying was my name, over and over and over.'

'I thought she was talking to him,' the girl said. 'I thought his name was Paul too.'

'Ah . . .'

'What did you see in the townhouse? I want to know.'

'I saw Martina's sombrero, hanging on a nail. That's it, and some graffiti next to it.'

'So be it?'

After a long pause, Paul said, 'How did you guess?'

'Do you believe in demons?'

'What kind of question is that?'

'Just what I said.' Her voice was still very young. 'Do you believe in demons?'

'Do you?'

'I asked first.'

'I believe,' Paul said, 'that if we don't believe in demons, they won't believe in us. Do the demons believe in us? That's the question. The day the demons believe in us, we're in real trouble.'

Martina's phone rang and cut off before either of them could find it. The number read 'withheld'. Late one weekend afternoon, the house lights came up all at once, the fridge shivered, a country ballad on the radio kicked in during its chorus. Paul whooped, 'Yee-haw!' and took the hammer to the shopping trolleys still lying around the site from the water runs and retrieved their coins. They ran to the supermarket and bought oats, nuts and syrup to bake flapjacks. The girl and her mother had always baked flapjacks, and Paul figured making flapjacks might liven up the place.

'How are you since?'

The old biddy in the supermarket was handing back their change in coppers when she asked that. Since what? Like they were compadres, Paul spat on the hard shoulder home, like they had ever even conversed about fucking anything.

Paul sat at the table watching his daughter, saying how like her mother she was getting. He told her how gorgeous she was, a young woman almost, how tall she was becoming. He thought he could smell burning. There was, as well, in the core of his skull, like a wasps' nest ablaze, this sizzle that he could scarcely hear his own voice above.

'You're not going to just disappear on me too,' he said, almost shouting. 'Are you?'

'No chance.'

'What?'

'I said no chance!' The girl was shouting too. 'I'm not going to just disappear!'

All the while, she was setting the timer on Martina's phone and wiping the mixing bowl, the spoons, tying her curls into a crushed-velvet scrunchie and watching through the oven's glass door. Once, she turned and smiled, the way her mother used. All the rooms were pure gold, with the bulbs still on and sun out the back. She was wearing only Martina's silk scarf as a bikini top and sweatpants that were far too loose on her. Her abdomen was exposed, the white crease marks that the elastic of her knickers cut in her skin, the twin pelvic bones like a pair of dainty fists covered with a cotton handkerchief. Just when they looked golden, perfect, the power died. The long-range weather forecast cut off *in medias res*, the fridge released a death rattle and all the rooms returned to the old gold of natural light. She said, 'I'm pretty sure they're done anyway.'

She divided the tray into twenty careful rectangles, three cuts lengthways and four widthways, the tip of her tongue on the chapped point of her upper lip, and rested each separately with the butter knife on a rack to cool.

'About ten minutes,' she said.

She said it again, walking into the front room. She said it from the bottom of the stairs.

'They're done,' she said. 'Ten minutes to cool.'

She stopped around the middle step. *Everybody turn*, the kitchen started bleating, *Everybody turn . . .*

'Papa? Please.'

She put her head around each bedroom door, saying his name as she did. She stood at the foot of the ladder and spoke into the attic's black square.

'Please, Papa, please.'

Both front and back doors were still locked from the inside. It was then, she said, that she started screaming, 'Papa, please! Papa, please!' It was then that she couldn't find the keys, that she heard them rattling in the pocket of her father's jacket and unlocked the front door's bolt from within and sprinted without breathing or stopping until she reached a door, which she hammered on and which I, finally, held open.

5

YOU KNOW THOSE stories, where the child is lost in the wilderness and presumed dead? For years her family keeps returning. Eventually, their hope dwindles. The family disintegrates: the mother remarries, the father lives alone. Then a creature wanders into the nearest village, semi-feral and with scant language. The villagers form a circle and stare. Someone asks questions she doesn't answer, or can't. Someone else remembers the family who came on holiday many moons ago and lost a daughter in the mountains, who kept returning to find her. One man, who had been acquainted with the family, had been employed as a guide even, recalls the girl's name, and the sound the name's word makes when said aloud is met by a flicker of recognition in her.

That's what it was like. It was as if she had come running, for all she was worth, out of some urban legend or 'real life' story in one of those magazines you read in a doctor's waiting room. The first door she happened on was mine, and she banged on that, and sat with me in my front room, and waited for the law to arrive, and answered a few routine lines of enquiry, and agreed to accompany us all back to her house.

'Sorry,' I said.

The older one in plain clothes, who appeared to be in charge, squinted slightly in my direction.

'I had to say something to the ladies at the gate,' I said.

Still he said nothing, and still I felt obliged to explain myself for some reason, in spite of that little voice inside pleading with me to stop apologizing.

'Sorry for keeping you.'

Because of the barriers the builder called Flood had erected across the entrance to the close, we left the cars outside and pushed our way through. It was still good and bright. The girl had the key so tight in her hand, since bolting from the house, that its ridges left sore-looking imprints inside her fist. It didn't matter: the front door to her house was still open.

I was the only one who stayed outside, by my own choosing.

'I'll wait outside,' I said.

'If you're sure.'

'Sure,' I said. 'I'd only be in the way.'

I could hear the officers shouting into each of the rooms before entering. Every once in a while I glimpsed shapes flitting across a window, and torchlight piercing those spaces that were shaded from the setting sun. It may be the exaggeration of hindsight, but there did seem to be something about the place. Call it an air, an eerie soundlessness, if you will. They were in there a good quarter of an hour and, in all that while, standing waiting on the bricks of their dusty drive, I scarcely heard a peep from the town or the ring road or its Saturday-evening traffic. The site was an absolute state, no tar laid, rubble everywhere, windows with holes in them, doors gaping, scraps of plastic and wiring and chalkboard, the skeleton of a car ploughed into a hill of muck. The charred shell of a caravan, which presumably had been there once for security, sat up towards the buildings that were meant to be flats. What if he came back? What if the father were to materialize there and then, only to find me whistling at the end of his drive and his daughter indoors with officers of the law I had summoned?

I stepped up to the door and beckoned through. 'Any joy?'

The door had partly pushed aside vast drifts of mail, as if the house had been deserted for years. There was also a repossession notice on the door, and all the doors for that matter, a white bill glued to the wood with a warning in red print not to remove it. The hall was black. The frame of a racing bike leaned against one of its walls. The interior smelt of nothing but dust and sunscreen lotion. Through the back windows, even though they were smeared with dirt, I could just about make out a couple of sun-loungers and a layer of grey parched muck where a lawn should have been.

I shouted again, 'Anything?' There was even a moment, mad as it sounds, when I wondered if anyone would ever re-emerge from that house. I had left with them to go in search of the girl's father. How would I explain returning alone to the ladies at my gate? 'Hello . . . ?'

I stepped out again to the end of the drive, trying to see into the upstairs windows. Finally, I heard voices and saw shadows preceding them back through the door.

'Nothing.'

The female officer made a face in my direction – a kind of wince. The girl had put a couple of things in a bag that had the crest of some designer outlet on it. She still had on her father's jacket: she had, it appeared, refused to change into something of her own. They were all of them, I remember, covered with sweat when they stepped out: beads on foreheads, and jackets removed, and shirt sleeves matted to skin.

'What will happen now?' I asked.

She was looking straight at me, the officer, mouthing: 'I haven't the foggiest.'

We all came back to my house. Things had quietened down at the supermarket. Mercifully, there was nobody waiting at my gate. The girl sat sniffling in front of the evening's programmes and being comforted. I boiled and reboiled the kettle, made several pots of tea that were never even poured, and the men in plain clothes alternated between ringing for instructions from superiors or relevant services and quizzing the girl. The same stuff, over and over again. Was there anywhere her father might have gone? Were there relatives? The girl said her grandparents, the father's folks, had gone away. She didn't know where, but it transpired that they were on a pilgrimage in Medjugorje.

'What about the sister?' It was me who asked that. I had kept my mouth shut, or as good as, until then. The girl had made no mention of her mother's sister, and the officers appeared to have forgotten momentarily. 'Wasn't there a sister?'

'We've asked her that already,' the younger woman officer said. 'Over in the house.' She looked amused by my involvement. 'She says Martina and her daddy had a row of some description. Martina went back abroad, isn't that right?'

'That's right,' the girl said.

'We'll be sure to chase it up.'

My telly was on mute in the background, a man picking lottery balls from a tube and placing them in a row on a rack, numbers facing outwards. They asked her about the writing on her skin.

'Writing?'

'The words on your skin. Did you write them yourself?'

'Yes.'

'And what do they say?'

The girl slowly opened the jacket she was wearing. She peered into the petite folds of flesh on her tummy. One by one, she ran a finger under each of the various smudged phrases.

'Words just.'

'What words?' The woman officer was doing all the talking. She was being very gentle, but insistent with it. 'Can you read me out some of the words?'

The girl glanced around at the four of us. It must have felt peculiar, being asked to read aloud to a roomful of strangers words inscribed on your body. It must have felt particularly peculiar to have all these grown-ups gazing at your naked flesh. Her flesh, where there was no ink or dirt, was perfectly unblemished. No goose-pimples or anything like that. It was red from the sun, and even inclined to brown in patches. It had the texture, her skin, of the pure fine suede of a peach. She peered down at herself once again and stretched her skin in various spots and spoke as if each word were acres apart from all the rest.

'This is it,' she said. 'Haze. Not quite the ticket. You are very good. Spring-loaded. Walkabout. There you are. So be it. On his plate. Heading up. Gilt.'

The younger of the detectives struggled to stifle a giggle.

The woman was giving him a filthy look. He had his elbows propped on his knees and started vigorously inspecting his interlocked fingers. The older one's phone went off in his shirt pocket. He took it outside.

'Do you mind if I have a look?' The woman was kneeling now. She had one of the girl's arms in her hand and was pushing the sleeve down from shoulder to wrist. The arm was criss-crossed with blue ink. 'What do the words mean?'

'Nothing,' the girl said.

'Nothing at all?'

'People said them and I wrote them to remember.'

The second detective summoned me into the hall. He used an odd phrase to do so: he said, 'If I could borrow you a sec.' I knew he meant me by the way he touched the elbow of my blazer. I drew the door behind me, assuming he didn't want the girl to hear whatever it was he had to tell.

'No luck with social,' he whispered on my doorstep. 'Saturday night, you know?' He shrugged and shook his head. He had, I remember now, a pipe that he lit then, out on my front step. 'This far off the beaten track,' he continued. 'Anywhere else, any other time of the week.' Still I said nothing. 'But placing her immediately could be tricky.'

It was as if he were leaving spaces, deliberately, for me to say what he wanted me to say. However determined I was not to say what he wanted, each space he left felt like a little vortex that I couldn't resist being sucked into.

'If needs really be,' I heard my own voice sighing, 'she can stay here. She'll be plenty safe.'

'We'll see.'

There was surprise in his voice when he said that. He even permitted himself a pursed smile. He had cornered me into offering something that I didn't want to offer and of which he was always going to disapprove. It never occurred to me that the girl would stay. It just seemed the proper thing to offer, being the nearest to her home, being the one she came to first.

'How old did you say she is?'

'I didn't,' I said. He was concentrating on his pipe. He couldn't seem to get a draw out of it. 'About twelve?'

'That young? Really?'

They all hung on for a couple of hours. At one point, there was talk of a bed for her in a care home in the capital, but that was over an hour's drive away and, besides, the girl seemed distraught at that idea of going far from her home. Two of them sat in the front room with her, the older detective and the uniformed woman, stepping outside every now and then to take a call. The third, the giggler, was sent off to wait in the car at the entrance to the site, in case anyone or anything turned up. Around eleven the pair of them asked me into my kitchen to inform me that there was no life on the close, no sign of her father. I told them I would ask my cleaner if the girl could stay with her for the night. They went in to talk to the girl, while I called my cleaner once more to ask her. Staying in the close, I could hear them explaining, wasn't an option.

'Your daddy will turn up tomorrow,' the female officer was promising. 'Nothing surer.'

'If he doesn't?'

'Let's not even go there.'

They waited till my cleaner returned. When she arrived, she had an overnight bag, a maroon sports hold-all, slung over her shoulder. She held up the bag and said, 'If it's okay by everyone, I thought it would be less disruptive if I stopped here rather than her coming to ours.' When none of us said anything, she added, 'She'll get more peace here.'

That idea, of my cleaner being with us in the house over-night, seemed acceptable. In one way, I was as relieved as they were by her suggestion. In another, to be honest, I was put out by the suspicion implicit in their relief. All this was happening on my doorstep, with my blessing, and yet some-how that added up to me being not entirely trusted. I pointed out that the spare room, which was made up and in which the girl could sleep, had a door with a key that she could lock from within; meaning that she would be perfectly safe with or without my cleaner staying over. But the words, spoken out loud and in that order, may have sounded shrill.

The officers assured us that they would be back first thing in the morning. They spoke to the girl in the front room, explaining to her that my cleaner would be staying over with us. She just looked vacantly at them. They offered some further comforting blather and disappeared into the silvery darkness, their siren black and silent.

'Are you set?' I asked the girl. I remember wondering how much English she could really speak. 'Are you not wiped?'

After that, I let my cleaner bring her up to the spare room. She picked up the girl's bag of things fetched from her house, and with the other hand coaxed her up out of her seat. I sat where I was, listening to my cleaner talking softly, pragmatically, on the staircase, as if the girl were some acci-dent victim relearning to walk. My cleaner would take my room across from the girl's, I thought, and I would bunk on the couch downstairs. There was extra linen somewhere.

Eventually I could hear the door of the spare room clicking shut. I could even hear the girl's key twisting within. The staircase creaked once again.

'She's a bit wobbly, as you might expect,' my cleaner said. 'But she knows she's safe too.'

'You're as good.'

She had the hold-all on her shoulder again. She asked, 'Do you really need me to stay?'

'Not really,' I said. After my little speech in the kitchen, I had no option but to play indifference. The thought of her not stopping with us, however, made me sick to my stomach and inclined to panic. 'But having promised the officers . . .'

'I'll come over at the crack of, before anyone is up and about.' She laughed. 'I have nothing in the bag anyway. It was just to reassure her nibs.' Then she seemed embarrassed. 'One thing.'

'Yes?'

'She's in her flowers.'

'She's . . .?'

'. . . *in her flowers*?'

'Leviticus,' I said. 'I was never sure entirely what that meant.'

'You know . . .' She rolled her tongue around the inside of one cheek. 'Time of the month?' I put my face in my hands. 'But she assures me she's got towels or what-have-you.' I remember groaning. She said, 'It'll be grand.'

I say this in the interests of honesty. We led the law to believe, my cleaner and I, that she would stay over with us. I was honest in all other aspects of this nightmare. This was the one falsehood, and even then it was one by omission only. At no subsequent point, as far as I'm aware, did anyone think to ask either of us, separately, whether or not my cleaner had actually stopped over on that first night. Without ever agreeing or even discussing it, neither of us has seen fit to divulge that minor truth. She said goodnight very quietly, tiptoed to the door and left me to push its latch with the softest imaginable click. The beam of her people-carrier blanched the curtain and disappeared.

I sat a bit on my own, the telly on and the door of the front room open. The telly's benign white noise, its voices and gunfire and orchestral sweeps, might have been audible to the girl and possibly of some comfort. Every once in a while I hit 'mute' and listened. There wasn't a whimper from upstairs. I was used to having the place to myself. Oddly, her presence in the house and my care of her made for a loneliness that never otherwise had been the case. Desperate for some familiarity, I even tried calling my younger brother in Florida. It would have been still only early evening there. Back then, we still called one another out of the blue. Sometimes, if you caught him and his wife at the right time of their day, my brother would put it to speaker and we chatted while they ate. My call went straight to voicemail and threw me. I held on after the beep, but could think of no message and succeeded in leaving only what must have been my muffled breathing and my sitting room's static hiss.

I sat until I could keep my eyes open no longer, switched off all the power points and stood alone in the murk of the downstairs hall. I think I even dabbed myself with water. I would never have been the nervous sort, but the thought of her up there in the room, able to step out at any moment and meet me on my own landing, gave me pause. I removed my shoes and put my faith in the soundlessness of the carpet's pile. I did wonder about tapping on her door and asking if everything was all right – it was so quiet – but I thought better of it. That might have scared her. Instead, I left the shaving light on in the bathroom, locked my own door as quietly as I could and lay in that magenta dark you get on a summer night.

I had known who she was when she appeared at my door. I knew the story inside out. There were the sisters' parents, going the way they did, and then the sisters emigrating. Their eventual return was big news locally, far more so than they seemed to be aware of. One of the sisters and the husband of the other twin got work in the new American factory. Some saw the quieter sister and her daughter, whom people said had a foreign accent, streeling around as if they were going to or coming from a beach that was nowhere near. Then the girl's mother's face was in the window of every shop and supermarket you stepped into, on telegraph poles all over the county. The story was reported everywhere initially, died away, and people did wonder: one minute she was this young mother back home to make a go of it with her family, the next she had vanished and there didn't appear to be much urgency about finding her.

I had walked over to the close, as they called it, a couple of times. Sheila and Harry were old friends of mine. It was Sheila who suggested that I pop up to number seven. She suggested it more than once, but at first I wasn't fussed. They were tomorrow's young, with their worldwide webs and their several languages. The last thing they wanted was yesterday's man on their doorstep, preaching ancient, hollow words. They weren't part of the congregation. They weren't really at Harry's removal or grave, though I did see the mother standing out on the close when Harry's coffin was being carried from the house. After the story broke, Sheila started saying it to me again and with ever greater insistence. She said she thought they would be glad of a friendly face, of a bit of counselling. In my position, it is expected. So I did; go up, that is. But I do remember feeling like an old fraud approaching their house, acting out a parody of my role, stalking souls in torment.

There was no answer. I pressed the bell three times, but still nothing. I was inclined to turn on my heels there and then, in the knowledge that I could tell Sheila I had tried. But I could hear life around the back, voices and music too, possibly from a radio. Before I ever got to the rear gate or made my presence known, I saw them through a sliver in the partition fence that went all the way down to the wall at the rear: the girl and a woman who was unusually fetching. They were drinking, talking in snatches, laughing. They were sunbathing, only their bottoms on – nothing else. The woman's skin was quite tanned, I remember, and basted in oil. They seemed oblivious of anything around them. I could have stayed there hours, unnoticed, gazing at their bare skin roasting. There is something about the flesh of young womanhood, a carnality so intensely consuming as to be almost ghostly. I could hardly draw my eyes away from it. But, as well as seeing them, I could also see myself watching them and how that would have looked to someone else who might have come along. So I backed away, my steps silent and my breath held. I turned and quickened only when I reached the end of their drive. Sheila had moved into her daughter's by then. There wasn't another sinner around. When I got out onto the open road, I did something I hadn't done in years and haven't since: I ran.

She was back, the mother. That's what I thought, completely forgetting about the sister. I thought the woman I had spied on, sunbathing topless in their unseeded garden, was the woman who had disappeared. After the initial fuss, the coverage and the lull, the same young mother had come back with little or no ceremony, and with an explanation so simple as to be embarrassing. There they were, basking in it, like lizards, and word of her return had simply never reached my ears. I said it to my cleaner one of the mornings she was in.

'That family,' I said, 'whose mother disappeared.'

'In the new development out the road?'

'She came back?'

'Did she?'

'I'm asking you.'

My cleaner had heard nothing. She asked me, 'Why do you say so?'

I could hardly say because I had seen them sunbathing topless in their garden, but I hadn't worked out another story, and I blushed and rustled the paper she had brought. She could see that it was in my head. She seemed amused and wouldn't let it go.

'What makes you think that?'

'Oh, just . . .'

It came up again, a couple of days later. My cleaner had asked around. We had forgotten about a sister, identical to her, living with them and taken up with her brother-in-law. I sighed when she added that last part.

'Taken up with?' I asked, in spite of my best efforts not to.

'A regular couple,' she said. 'That's what they're saying.'

She was always doing that, invoking some faceless plural to lend substance to flimsy word-of-mouth. Those moments that she did so were the closest we ever came to quarrelling. In all other respects, my cleaner was a dream. If I am honest with myself, I would have to say that since I was probably a little soft on the woman I had seen sunbathing, I was hurt on her behalf by those rumours.

'*They* being?' I asked. The annoyance in my voice should have been plain. 'The idle of the parish?'

'The sister might well be still alive,' my cleaner said, seemingly heedless of my tone. 'Be a right mess if she does come back.'

I let it go. I confess that I was fascinated. That was as far as it ever went. What form did that fascination take? I would go out of my way to drive by the house, would slow past the close and look up. You would see the father and daughter traipsing back from the town with water bottles in bulk. I thought of stopping to ask them if they wanted a lift home, the girl and the father, who had started to look thin and dishevelled. The sister was never with them. I confess, too, since I wish more than anything now to be completely honest, that I did look up the local papers in the reference section of the library. I did get copies of the reports. But I wasn't the only one and I never pretended otherwise, though there was a time when the small fact of my interest in them was treated like a huge secret revealed under duress. It was just fascination. At the very worst, it was prurience. Was I guilty of prurience? Possibly. And for that I am ashamed. But prurience definitely is as far as it ever went.

*

I scarcely slept a wink that night. All of it was churning in my head. There were moments, too, when I was convinced that I could hear rummaging across the landing. Once, even, I got up to make sure that my bedroom door was locked, and I stood in darkness trying to hear noises other than my own creaks and those that are normal for any house at night. After hours lying motionless, I rose at five, dressed without washing, crept down in stockinged feet to where my shoes were waiting on the bottom step and let myself out the back door. It was late in August by then and not quite light. There was an edge of cold to it, suddenly, and talk of the weather breaking. Leaving the girl alone and locked inside a house that was strange to her was probably wrong, but my cleaner would be over within a couple of hours, I knew that, and the relief of getting out of there was huge, and the sharp autumnal nip felt beautiful. I was never so happy, or early for that matter, going about my Sunday-morning routine as I was then.

The girl was at the table when I got back around eleven. The radio was doing its usual gentle round-table prattle. My cleaner was there, as good as her word, removing her apron as I stepped in. She asked me, 'Everything okay?'

'Everything's fine,' I said. 'Here?'

'We're all fine here.' There was a forced clarity to my cleaner's voice when she said this. She glanced over at the girl gazing at a plate. Then she said, with reproach in her tone, 'When I came in, Madam was sitting at the table. Heaven knows how long she'd been there. So we said we'd get the breakfast going.'

'I had to go over early to do some things,' I said. 'Did we

sleep?' Not a word of answer. I asked my cleaner, 'Anything from the station?' The idea of a day alone with her nibs was not something I wished to countenance. 'Word of any sort?'

'Not a thing.' She had on her best jacket. 'I'll look in later on.'

'You're very good.'

After she left, the girl started eating. She had, for some reason, been waiting for it to be just ourselves. Her eating was memorable for one thing: she ate her breakfast with a spoon. Sausages, rashers, eggs, the works. She ate them all with a spoon and with the ferocity of someone who had not smelt hot cooked food in weeks. She devoured it, even using her hands at times.

'Take your time,' I told her.

I was laughing when I said that. I was saying it only to hide my embarrassment, and hers. She was finished within minutes, before I was even halfway through my own breakfast. I placed one of my sausages on her plate.

'Go on,' I said. 'Did they not feed you up in that close?' I regretted, immediately, the way it made my view of their circumstances obvious; and that thoughtless past tense, as if she would never be back there. She didn't touch the sausage at first. 'I'll butter some bread,' I said, clinking the tip of my knife off the edge of her plate. 'You eat that.'

She was very touching. She was just a small girl. I felt immediately protective of her. Where part of me did not want her there, another part wanted her never to leave. After a certain age, a man has to work hard to look trustworthy. That's even truer in this vocation. You want desperately to prove to the world that you are not like that, however much the world assumes you are. You put yourself in the way of danger to prove that you still can be. Trusted, I mean. It's like those old movies where the lost wastrel is taken in by the decrepit recluse and each is changed for the better. I felt sufficiently sentimental about her to have had something of that nature in my head. I felt, also, that it might help to treat her like my own as long as she was there – to give her some routine, some solidity.

'Bath,' I said. 'You have clean things?'

'Is there water?'

That was another oddity. She seemed preoccupied with water, its availability, its whereabouts, as if she had just returned from the missions.

'Hot water?' I said. 'There's loads.' She looked puzzled. More than that, I would say. She looked amazed. 'Give yourself a good long soaking. And don't appear back down until you're a sight cleaner than you are.'

That was the first time she smiled. That is, in my company. She tucked her hair behind one ear and giggled a little. So I waved an ironic wave up and down in her direction, as if to say, 'You should take a look in a mirror.' Her skin, presumably, was still covered in blue ink. She struggled up from her chair, laughing more loudly. I remember the inside of her mouth: the bad state her teeth were in, the tongue parched grey.

'I see,' she said. 'I thank you.'

'Go.'

I thank you. That one went round and round in my head downstairs, as I tidied away the breakfast things, while the taps plashed water into the bath and her footsteps moved back and forth from her room. The taps stopped, the door shut, but the lock, I noticed, did not click. I sat on the last step of the stairs, hearing sudsy water sloshing and her staggered mothy singing in a foreign tongue. When she stood in the kitchen a while later, her black hair was wet and sleek, her skin much fairer than it had seemed before.

'Go on inside,' I said. 'You know how to work the remote?' She nodded to that. 'I'll keep trying the station to find out what's happening.'

She watched telly for most of the afternoon. It wasn't obvious that she was seeing what was on. The usual Sunday programmes came and went: hurling, cowboys, antiques . . . I worked, or pretended to, at the kitchen table littered with papers and documents that made me look far busier than I really was. I got no answer from the garda station, or from either of my cleaner's numbers. A couple of times I sat in and asked what she was watching. Shortly before tea, she appeared beside me in the kitchen. She wanted to know where she would be staying, said she needed to go over to the house to fetch her laptop. I couldn't see the harm of it, as long as she understood that she wouldn't be staying there. I tried calling the station again. This time someone did answer, the same eejit who had answered first time the previous night. I asked to speak to one of the officers. He said they were all off duty, but assured me that it was being dealt with and that someone would be coming for the girl that evening. I told him where we were headed and for how long. This time, for some reason best known to your man, my call was not logged. They would later claim I had made no contact with them. Mercifully, my phone record told a different story.

*

We parked, as we had the previous evening, at the entrance to the close, pushed through Flood's wire barrier and walked the hundred yards or so up to the house.

'I'll wait out here.'

'I want you to come in,' she said.

The drifts of post were there from the previous day: dozens of official-looking letters, flyers for pizza delivery, council notices, free local newspapers, cards for tradesmen, charity sacks for cast-offs that had been due for collection months before, trial subscriptions and credit offers nobody had ever requested, legal warnings with red stamps and one handwritten note in green biro on a piece of blue-lined paper torn raggedly from a copybook, all crushed up against the bottom step of the stairs. We kicked through them like snow. A standard-ration telephone sat upside-down, its wires unplugged and spooled around it. On the mantelpiece was a framed photo of an elderly couple. They had their arms around one another, beaming, but the skyline in the background looked very far away. Some of the bits of furniture, like a glass coffee-table with a chrome fruit bowl, had obviously survived from the show-house days. Around them, in the front room, lay the flotsam of a family's life: a large telly with wire spaghetti and boxes underneath; two cheap acrylic beanbags with the impressions of having been sat in recently; cobwebs and popcorn crumbs. In the far corner was a stack of rubbish that looked as if it had come from some student's bedsit: a dismantled computer table with a maple veneer; a metal filing cabinet the colour of putty and a tower of empty drawers next to it; several football posters all scrolled into one; a sleeping bag bulging out of its shiny sleeve and a wafer-thin black dartboard with yellow numbers.

The worktop in the kitchen didn't have a spare inch on it, with tins of beans and apricots bought in bulk, and bottles of water still cellophaned together and warm to the touch. The sink was heaped with unwashed plates, pots and cutlery, patches of fuzz and mould, a stench like someone had got sick and never mopped it up. I had to concentrate hard on not looking as horrified as I felt. A picnic table had two matching plastic chairs at it, and two other chairs stacked in the corner beside a wicker basket full of junk. The windows were so filthy as to be almost opaque. The door out onto the patio was bolted. The back garden's stubble was littered with poppies and empty wine bottles. Out in the middle, marooned in no man's land, were the two cheap white plastic sun-loungers situated parallel to one another.

Everything was caked in orange dust off the building site: the windows, the furniture, the bottles and tins, their packaging, even the dirty dishes in the sink, the loungers out the back, the envelopes in the hall. I had only to run one finger along the nearest thing and my fingertip's skin came up red-black and the thing's surface gleamed all over again. I could taste the dust coating the inside of my mouth, like paprika left out for years and gone stale, flavourless. Or it was like being in a house on some volcanic island where the residents – however hard they showered on the deck, and removed all footwear upon entrance, and swept religiously – couldn't stop the ash bleeding into the house.

'I'll wait here,' I called. I was in the kitchen. The girl had already disappeared above. 'You won't take ages, will you?'

Outside was getting very gloomy, what with nights starting to close in and a bank of cloud that looked as if it might overspill. None of the light switches worked. The taps yielded no water. It was unaccountably clammy. I parked in a chair at their picnic table, removed my blazer, unbuttoned my collar and rolled up my shirt sleeves as far as they would go. On the glass of the patio window there seemed to be the faint outline of letters drawn in the dust ages before with someone's finger, but the words the letters formed were no longer legible.

How long was I there? Probably not as long as it seemed, but long enough for it to get fairly murky. I climbed the stairs to hurry her along. She was talking, chirpily enough it has to be said, up in the attic. I walked in and out of the bedrooms. A stale, dry air hung in them, of dirty laundry strewn all over the floors and beds, of trashy novels gauzed in the dust of hair and dead skin. The fitted wardrobes in the master bedroom had been stripped of their doors, and hanging there were all the mismatched colours of her mother's clothes. The single mattress was gone from the bed in the girl's room. On the futon in the box room there was an open laptop with purple dog-eared Post-its around its margins and a screen coated in dust. I remember, most of all, a round hairbrush on a stool, full of long black curls that must have been the sister's. When I picked it up, it smelt of coconut.

The ladder, one of those rickety telescopic aluminium jobs propped into the attic's trap, wobbled under my weight. I could just about discern the outline of two mattresses, sheets and sleeping bags in disarray around them. I could smell old candles, though there was no flame, and something like an orange decomposing. She was at the other end, seated upright against the breeze blocks, legs crossed yoga-style under her, the bulb of the laptop's screen making her face's contours a vivid sapphire. She was saying, 'Nein,

nein . . .' and a second distorted voice responded in kind against a background of flak that was like a dog barking away off in a valley. There was also what sounded like rain on the slates above us. When she saw me, she said, '*Ein sec,*' and the laptop hushed.

'Are we set?' I did my best to clear the tremble from my own voice.

'What?' She looked in my direction, but her eyes were without focus and her gaze was more past me than at me. I put it down to the light from her screen and the strange half-silhouette I must have appeared to her, climbing out of an underworld that was scarcely brighter than hers.

'Are we fit, ready?' I wasn't sure if she was getting a single word I was uttering. 'You can bring that with you.'

'Bring what with me?'

'Your computer. Bring it with you and we'll make tracks.'

The second I disappeared from view, there was laughter and then the voices resumed their chirping. Her mother was long gone. There was no mention of her auntie. The previous afternoon, her father had vanished as well. Not twenty-four hours ago, she'd appeared at my door in a blind panic. Now she was up there chewing the fat with whom-ever, laughing, as if none of this had happened. I slumped back on the same chair that my blazer was on, and resolved to wait there. It was indeed trying to rain outside. Huge sweat drops were bouncing off the weeds' leaves, forming rivulets down the double-glazing.

There are moments when the empty space of a room takes on the shape of one who must have stood there and who perhaps should still be there. In those moments, that space is like a cavity, an entrance even. It hangs heavy with absence. Its translucence collects, magnifies. Everything the other side of it appears minutely out of proportion with everything else outside its frame. It acquires a quality. There is no other word for it. The quality the empty space acquires is that of a lake's surface or of some lead-based mirror glass. It feels as though you could almost reach forward and dip your bare hand in it, through it, until your hand disappears up to the wrist. So it was that late afternoon – sitting waiting for the girl to come back down, her distant murmuring in a strange tongue, the scent of sun oil so strong as to be almost tangible, the garden's clay at last blackening with falling rain – that the shape the room's empty space took before me seemed to belong to one or other sister. So much so that I even stood up from my white picnic chair, that I approached, that I reached my shaking hand out towards it, that I even spoke.

'Yes?'

To what? Something that was surely not there or, rather, nothing that did appear to be. If I concentrated hard enough, I could simply step forward and slip into it as into some interior quarter. I, too, could enter its thin air.

'What are you doing?'

The girl had been watching from the threshold between the kitchen and the hall, a fresh hoodie on her. She looked frightened, of me. How I must have appeared, standing there sleeved in perspiration, one arm outstretched, trying to come into contact with little other than the humid murk of that dishevelled kitchen.

'I saw a spider,' I said. I was mortified. 'I think I got it.'

She walked around me, hands pouched in her hoodie. She drifted, indeed, on purpose it seemed, across the empty space I had been reaching out to, into the front room and back again. She touched nothing. She just looked at things. She studied them even, as though she had never glimpsed any of them before. She peered longest at the photo of the couple on the mantelpiece. She eventually said, 'George and Georgina.'

'Your mother's parents?'

'No,' she said. 'They were here when we came.' She was speaking in the plural still, albeit a past-tense plural. 'We called them George and Georgina.'

I remember thinking how slight and isolated her presence was, wandering around the rooms her parents and her auntie had once filled with limbs and voices, pausing now and then in some sort of recognition, steeling herself to be brave, conceding all those inanimate objects to the immediate past.

'I'm ready for leaving,' she said.

'Laptop?'

'Don't need it.'

'I thought that's what we came for.'

The rain was torrential. She flipped her hood up in the porch, I pulled my blazer above my head, and we both dashed to my car. I had to set the wipers to top speed and the fan at full blast to demist the windscreen. I asked her who she had been talking to in the attic. She said it was her best friend. She said, 'You?'

'Me?' I knew what she meant and she recognized that she had no need repeating the question. 'I thought there was someone else in the room. For a second.'

'That happens.'

She went up to my spare room, the one she had slept in the first night. She went up at my instruction to get out of her sopping clothes. She had little else to change into. I knew that, and left a bundle of my own bits folded on the floor of the landing. I put fish fingers under the grill. I set to making a small coal fire in the front room. It had been months since the hearth was lit. But it had turned unexpectedly chilly, and I thought the idea of a fire might comfort the girl. When I spun away from the flame, she was standing beside my upright piano, combing her wet hair with her fingers.

'Jesus,' I said. I don't remember ever swearing like that. 'I didn't hear you come in.'

'Sorry.'

She wore only the sweatshirt I had left out, one with 'Virginia' printed across the breast that had been a gift from my brother years before, when he was a law student over there. The sweatshirt fell almost to her knees. Below its hem her legs were bare and bore a couple of bruises. The sleeves were dangling well beyond her fingertips. She held her arms out, one at a time, and I rolled each cuff several turns until her wrists were visible.

'What did your dad and your mam's sister fight about?'

I had wanted to ask that several times before then, but had thought better of grilling her with questions, like all the others, and squandering whatever morsel of trust I had won. She was saying something about a hairdryer, I think, when I asked her this. At first, I thought she might not have heard. Or that she had heard and was choosing to ignore. Then she said, 'Nothing.'

'Nothing?' When she didn't answer that, I forced the issue. 'What does *nothing* mean, Helen?'

'There was no fight,' she said. 'She just went out and never came back. A month ago.'

'You should have told that to the officers.' I wasn't cross with her, but I may have sounded as if I was. 'You should have told them that your auntie was gone missing too.' I was more horrified. I slumped onto the piano stool. 'What possessed you to lie to them?'

'Papa said to tell nobody. People might think there was something wrong with us.'

It was at that point that she wept openly. Her face creased into itself and plump tears streamed down. She rubbed the knuckles of her index fingers into her eyes, the way a baby does, instinctively. She even sat down on my knee. Just like that. I don't believe she realized what she was doing. We stayed in that position for several minutes. I could feel her thin bones through my slacks. I could smell her shampoo's coconut scent. She was heavier than you might have expected, as if all the secrets she had inherited added to her weight.

I wanted to hold her head in my hands. Instead I sat frozen, like one carrying some invisible globe, while her hair fell around her bent head and her whole frame shook. I shooed her towards the swelling fire and washed my hands with carbolic soap at the sink. Her sobs were still audible above the kettle's singing. I stepped back in with a tray bearing mugs and a plate of fish-finger sandwiches.

'Now,' I said.

We could hear the rain still hammering outside. At first, I didn't know where to put myself. Nobody came or called, much as we waited. Nobody picked up in the garda station the couple of times I dialled, or at either of my cleaner's numbers.

'I want to stay here again.'

'Not a hope.'

I was pleased with myself for making that much clear. We dragged a pair of easy chairs to either side of the hearth, ate off our laps and set in for a vigil of sorts. I remember the buttery tomato sauce that squeezed out and dribbled between her fingers, which she licked clean. I remember how, when she had finished, she wiped her hands dry on the sweatshirt; her fascination with the fire, the way she sat forward, elbows on knees and poker dangling, watching its flurries and lulls, prodding crevices in the slack for evidence of life; the way she shivered and lifted coals carefully, one by one, with the tongs. She had, she said, seen Slattery do it and had been dying to ask for a go.

'So the Slatterys had you up?'

'Freaks,' she said.

'*Freaks.*' I said it in such a way as to suggest that she was being uncharitable, though I knew she was right.

'That's what Papa called them.'

'Take this.' I had poured two thimblefuls of brandy and handed one to her. 'My mother used always give us this for shock or toothache or the like.'

'Is she still alive?'

'My mother?' I was laughing. 'Lord, no!'

That was the only prompt she needed. She just launched forth and, when I never once made to interrupt, she kept going. The more she spoke, the more fluent she became. The metallic edge seemed to wear off her voice while she talked, staring forward, her features flushed in the glow. I heard everything she had not mentioned to the officers: the hours devoted to sunbathing; the words on the back window;

the puzzled email from Ute that her auntie left open on a screen; her mother walking across the garden in a bridesmaid's dress on the same evening that the girl had heard her father and auntie in the bedroom . . .

'Martina said they were just talking,' she said. 'But they weren't.'

'You don't know that.'

'She went all red when she found me outside the room. And her hands were wet.'

There was a sliver of anger in her voice when she said that last bit. The auntie had resumed her visits to the security lad, Marcus. Neither the girl nor her father ever alluded to her nightly absences. One night the auntie didn't come home and her father searched the townhouses. The builder, Flood, said the lad had been in Reading for weeks. They told no one that her auntie was gone. Her father was made redundant. Slattery invited them to his house and knew everything about them. The feeling that someone else was present had driven them up into the attic this past month, scared stiff. She even acted out the exchange that she and her father had had in the darkness of the attic. She said she had asked him about demons because of all the noises they kept hearing.

'Noises?'

'Noises,' she said. 'The wall banging from the empty house joining ours. The Poles in number three.'

'The Poles?' I knew for a fact that number three had remained vacant since Sheila had moved in with her daughter.

'Papa called them that,' she said. 'I never saw them.'

I remember her small hands cupped around the

tumbler, the look of worry on her face whenever I thought I heard the phone ringing and raised one finger to stall her story, the way she could scarcely bring herself to utter some of it and giggled through other stuff, such as Slattery's airs and war booty. Her teeth were a little bucked, though only in a way that added to her prettiness, and stuck out whenever she was amused. She would tilt her head, at lengthy regular intervals, to get her hair dry. The skin of her jawline, throat and breastbone was so pure and pale. After the amusement subsided, her fire-bound gaze clouded over and she resumed precisely where she had tapered off.

It is possible, as I say, that I heard more than she said; or that my memory has added to her telling those details that I wanted to hear but which the girl could not have witnessed or imparted. But I do still believe she saw far more than her family realized. And I think part of me recognized something of my own means of inhabiting the world in her description of herself. In every episode she was the faceless, ever-present bystander, marginal to the point of being overlooked, but observing and absorbing everything. She was there all along – you could say we both were – and yet had gone too easily unnoticed. I was even inclined to wonder if she recognized something of the same in me. I remember wishing I could offer her more in the way of shelter, being touched by her and wanting her to feel as touched.

At some point in that late evening, during the unbroken spell in which she spoke and I listened, the dial tone of the landline died. I must have walked to the stand in the hall and back a dozen times. No line at all, either coming in or going out. Even my mobile yielded only an uninterrupted drone whenever I pressed the 'call' button. We sat waiting until some ungodly hour, in the hope that a car would pull up. I didn't want her to stay. It was not safe, as much for me as for her. I stood in the porch, peering at the deluge, as if attempting to will the world back to us. There were already huge pools along the edges of the road. All the lights on the old road were blank, and there was not the slightest splash of traffic. In the distance, however, towards the town, there was a pink, wavering glow on the skyline and the faint echo of sirens. I even considered driving towards it. In a moment of panic I considered finding coats for us both, and making our way towards those echoes, that glow.

Finally, I shut the front door, blanked the porch light and headed back inside, knowing that there was nothing else for it but for her to stop a second night.

'Let's go,' I said.

I said it loudly, though it appeared then that she had only pretended to doze off. She dragged all her hair across one shoulder and twisted it with one fist into a loose spiral. When she faced away from the fire towards me, she seemed momentarily older somehow, no longer quite the child. So much so that I even stepped backwards. She rose and left the room, brushing past me as she did, forgetting to pretend to regain consciousness as well.

'We'll drive over to the station in the morning,' I called after her, 'and sort this once and for all.'

I remember setting the guard in front of the fire, wedging it firmly with the poker. The handle of the poker was still clammy from her grip. I lifted her tumbler off the tiles of the hearth. She had taken only a few sips and most of what I had poured for her was still sitting in it. There were marks on the rim where she had sipped. I remember holding that tumbler against the light of the fire's remnants and being able to make out the shape of her lips, her smears of saliva and breadcrumbs; inhaling the musk off her drink; positioning my own lips where hers had marked the glass, and keeping them there. It was lukewarm, her drink was, sweet, like the dregs of red lemonade left overnight. I remember the scorch of it on my tongue and in my throat when I finally threw my head back and swilled and knocked off all the power points.

'Can I sleep in your room?'

She was on the landing. She had her head bowed, her hair down around her face. She had the cuffs of my sweat-shirt rolled back down and bunched around her fists. She was shivering. I said something like, 'Ah, here.' I was at my wits' end. I did want to protect her, but I needed to protect myself too. There was always going to be a reckoning, some-where down the line, and I was wise enough to realize even then that I would have this truth to tell.

'We can drag the mattress over,' she said, still looking downwards. 'I can sleep on your floor, like I used do with Papa.'

'Not a hope.' I was snorting light-heartedly when I said it, letting her down as softly as I could manage. I was trying to shepherd her towards her own space. 'Not a hope in hell.'

'Please, Father.' I'll never forget it, how she said that. 'Please.'

I held open the door of the room in which she had slept the night before and nodded inwards. 'Let's go.'

She tiptoed through her own things scattered around the floor. I folded back the sheets that she must have straight-ened from the previous night and she curled beneath the bedding, my sweatshirt still on her. I remember gathering her saturated clothes, leaving them to dry on the footboard and standing bedside.

'Now,' I said.

The rain was fairly pummelling down. I straightened out the hem of her sheet and blanket. She tucked her face below the edge of the fold, so that all you could see were her hair and the nape of her neck. I wanted to tell her that she was perfectly safe, to pat the back of her head and the hairline where black strands dissolved into white skin, to rub my thumb around that ball of bone at the top of her spine. Instead, I pulled her door behind me, switched off the landing light and twisted the key of my own lock as slowly as I could manage.

I did think about her. If I'm guilty of anything else, I'm guilty of that. I'm guilty of thinking about the girl in bed in the room across from my own. I am a man as well, after all. She was twelve, or so they said. But even then I wondered if she might have been more than that. She was as pitiful as she was pretty, and she was pretty in spades. There was something about that combination, at my mercy, that I could not help imagining. For the second time I lay in the dark across the landing from her. This time I was relieved to get that far away. I remember closing my eyes, sighing deeply and seeing my own mother walking towards me, on a track in a field next to our homeplace. I remember feeling very happy to see her, in sunlight there, inching towards me. I called something, but she didn't hear or understand. When she got nearer, I could see that she had 'Virginia' printed across her breast, and that her legs and feet were bare and covered with scratches.

'Father,' she was calling. To me. I remember puzzling, even in dream, how strange it was that our late mother should be walking towards me in a sweatshirt given to me by my brother, and that she should address me as such.

'Father.'

The handle and lock were rattling. How long had I been asleep? Three hours? The rain was still lashing outside. Ten minutes? I had no idea.

'Father, please.'

My own heart was pounding in my chest. She was just a child, I kept telling myself. She was a small soul in immense pain. I should have gone out to her, seen what the matter was.

'Father, please.'

But the thought of her grandparents and her missing parents had crossed my mind umpteen times by then. I knew little about the sister. Whoever was out there was the one who had survived them all and I, to my eternal shame, was too scared to go and face whatever demon was on my landing.

'Father? Please . . .'

She kept calling my name. My door shuddered, every once in a while at first, and then constantly for ages. I just lay there. If I'm guilty of one last thing, I'm guilty of just lying there, saying nothing and doing nothing. I was scarcely breathing, as if not breathing would make it recede. Even when her door slammed around dawn and I could have sworn I heard screaming, I did nothing. The screams were muted by the walls and wood between us, but they were clear enough and they were clearly hers.

She was gone the following morning. She was gone and

her made bed looked as if it had never been slept in. But that's not right, since 'gone' implies a where to be gone to. She wasn't anywhere. That's the way I have come to think of it, to phrase it. By the following morning she was nowhere, and I was the last to have seen her, and all hell broke loose.

6

'FROM THE BEGINNING,' he says. 'Tell us what you saw.'

It is the first one who says that, the older man in plain clothes who had taken the call out to my doorstep that first Saturday evening and tried to fix up something with social services. Curtin. That was his name. By which I mean his real name. For various reasons, the identities of all the others have been protected. By virtue of being definitively no longer with us, he is the only character in any of this who goes by his real name. Which is odd, considering how other-worldly his presence sometimes felt. Curtin. I must have been told his name more than once before, but it hadn't registered until then and there in that windowless room. The younger man, the one who had sniggered at the words on the girl's skin, sat slightly outside the lamplight. I never caught his name, or perhaps it was never told to me properly. On the table between us microphones were propped on mini-stands. There was also the red pinhead glow that told us we were being recorded.

Possessing copies of our exchanges was an entitlement that I, at my brother's insistence, exercised. My brother acted on my behalf, to some extent. His training was overseas, under a different jurisdiction. He had also retired by then. But we spoke several times on the phone during those autumn months. And he communicated with Curtin, informally, on my behalf. The one thing my brother was adamant about was that I – or 'we' as he preferred to phrase it – should receive copies of all recorded interviews. So I have them still, on discs in a see-through plastic tub the size of a shoebox, in an upstairs room that acts as an office. Mostly, I let them gather dust on the shelf there. Nowadays, whenever I play them back, it is against my better self. Mostly, I get free of it and forget. Then, for whatever reason, memory stirs. I pull down the recordings, sit late listening in sequence, and then feel hung-over for days.

It is Curtin who is always first to speak. There is the clunk of the thing, the mechanism, switching into life. There is paper rustling. There are always the shrieks of chairs being pushed away for extra legroom. Then Curtin speaks. He says the time and date and place. He itemizes those present. His voice, all business, is not entirely his. It is excessively pronounced, clipped, delivering archival information. Then, after a few throat-clearing coughs and snuffles, his more relaxed northern gravel kicks in.

'In your own time so,' he says. 'Tell us everything you remember seeing.'

The truth I maintained then was almost exactly the same as it is now. I saw nothing. I heard plenty, far more probably than I should have, and I have recounted faithfully everything I heard. Much has been said and reported, by others, about what happened. Some of that is true, and other parts are pure fairy tale, or at least according to what I know. And, yes, much of this account exceeds what I could possibly have seen or heard. It has, I accept, merely blossomed in the rubble of years between those events and my remembering of them. Perhaps too much has been said. But now, for what shreds of my dignity I still possess and for my fragile peace of mind, I need to make this one truth clear: I saw next to nothing.

How long ago is this? Lately, I find it hard to tell. There are days now when it feels like this happened to someone else and that I, too, am merely one of those who read about it in the papers or who caught it on the evening bulletin. There are days when it feels as if all this happened in a whole different century, and in a place very far from here. That last part is correct. I am not 'here' any more. I am writing from elsewhere. I hope never to be posted in that place again. For a long time, now and then, in company, I would be asked to repeat my name and my face would grow familiar. There was a phase when I felt famous even, when crowds parted where I walked and friends muttered to one another and shutters clicked. Mostly, in company long after, an element of tact would register around me. There would be twitches, a change of subject, while those who accidentally found themselves in my presence figured out an acceptable angle of approach or, more often, of withdrawal.

Odd times, though rarely, some careless twit would puncture that tact by blurting, 'Weren't you the guy who . . . ?'

I was never greatly bothered by the eejits, the blurters. In many respects, they were infinitely preferable to the mortified dumbstruck majority.

'Yes,' I would say. 'That was me.'

They always came back to the same question: 'What was she like?' And I always resorted to the safest equation.

'What was she like?' I would say. 'She was like nothing on earth.' She was. 'Like nothing on earth.'

*

It is morning now, early autumn. Two sides of this building are bathed in light growing warmer and more vivid by the minute. Two sides are dew-damp terrace cushions and stone cold underfoot. Give it time, I tell myself each morning. Come evening, all will be reversed: those terrace cushions will feel dry to the touch and the palm fronds out front will cast no shadows. Meantime, the odd car or scooter buzzes along the dust track beneath the olive trees, bells gong in one of the hamlets down in the valley, a cacophony of dogs answers in staggered chorus and the peaks that form our nearest horizon sparkle with marble and quartz as if with snow.

Give it time. I am far from alone. There is a gardener who doubles as the Sunday-morning bell-ringer. I believe he knows all about me, though he and I have never really conversed. He materializes, in straw hat and braces, on slopes beneath the house. He heaps dead twigs and windfalls onto the compost midden, and covers all with cuttings of grass or leaf. There are some Saturdays when he flirts with the black-frocked ladies who dust down the tiny church for Sunday's only early mass. Those days he wears the suit he usually keeps for the Sabbath. He has a stick and a German shepherd.

'Ombra,' he once said to me.

I had carried into the sun a little table from the utility room. I was eating bread and jam, soaking in the first morning of real heat. He had appeared around the corner of the house. He was next to me before I knew he was there. My coffee cup rattled a little on its saucer, and his dog came sniffing at my feet.

'Ombra,' he said again, pointing to the dog.

'*Si*,' I replied at last, realizing that he was telling me the creature's name. 'Indeed.'

'Ombra,' he repeated. He came towards me and patted my shoulder. '*Molte ombre.*'

Here was a medieval monastery fallen into ruin when my landlady's father had bought it after the war. As children, they drove south through the night with their parents and spent every August here. The rest of the complex belongs to her brothers, but they never come. The *chiesa*, which my landlady subsidizes out of her cut of the family foundation, is open to the locals. She needs someone here year-round to keep the house from falling into disrepair and to maintain the immediate grounds in some semblance of order. Even she had heard where I had fallen from, that I was in need of a soft place to land. My name had been passed on to her by a friend of my brother, someone close to the hierarchy. I was visited, though not by her, to outline the arrangement. Then she wrote to me on headed notepaper, with a cursive hand in black ink that had already faded mauve by the time it was delivered. She said how pleased she was that I had agreed, though I had agreed to nothing. There didn't seem to be any choice in the matter. If I am honest, it gave me something to say to people, a future to describe that did not sound entirely without hope. She told me not to hesitate to ask if ever there was anything I needed, but left no details for reaching her. The ticket passed on to me was for a seat that was going spare on a chartered plane. I was met by my own name misspelt on a piece of cardboard and taxied up inland. A woman who had known my landlady from infancy was waiting on the step with keys and with no English. Her hair, I remember, was dyed ebony.

How long ago? Five years? I assumed that this would be a stop-gap, a halfway house on the path to another life. Five years at least, if not twice that, and no prospect of it ending. I pay no rent or bills. The meters are read remotely. I keep all post for my landlady in a wicker laundry basket inside the main door: it is overspilling. My shelves are well stocked with non-perishables, and once a week a box of fresh produce is delivered to the doorstep. I don't know where it comes from or who drops it off. There is no set time. However hard I try, however long I sit and watch in hope of passing the time of day, I never see them approach or leave.

I suspect it was my brother who requested that I be offered a role in the sacraments, and for that I am grateful. Sundays, the bell gonging in the valley is ours, us. The black-frocked ladies multiply. They climb the cobblestones in hats, bearing wildflowers hand-picked along the road as gifts for the holy well in the courtyard. A local cleric drives here from an adjacent parish in an antique black Mercedes. He conducts his masses like some crooner or matinee idol, swaying behind the pulpit, incanting the responsorial psalms. I serve. Though I remain familiar with few of their words, I am well able to follow the rhythm of the sacraments. I take a second chalice. I mutter, '*Il corpo di Cristo.*'

'Amen,' the ladies sing back. Like egrets, they open their mouths to receive.

Afterwards, while he babbles all his news in the vestry, I fold my borrowed cassock and return it to the red sports bag in which he carries his things. The glare outdoors is intense. The locals chat under the trees for another hour; though they live on the same mountain, presumably this is the only time of the week they meet. I shade my eyes and sidle through my door. I hear their voices, their laughter, bubble and ebb. I hear their valedictions.

The other six days of the week revert to being mine and mine alone. I do odd jobs, to keep my hand in, to justify my presence. I take a power hose to the cobbles. I keep the woodshed stocked. I prune the younger of the olive orchards. I shoulder a chainsaw to where a pine has fallen in my forest and make logs of it and fill a trailer. Odd days a flock of pilgrims in hiking boots will ask for directions, or a newly married couple will have their wedding snaps taken among my groves, or some unfortunate will beat a track to my door selling matchboxes off the bar of his bicycle. After the sun falls suddenly, I draw all drapes to block out the dark and make up a daybed for myself just off the kitchen. But there are nights, I confess, when it catches up with me again. I bring down the box of discs. I listen to myself. Not everything, or not everything any more. Time was I could listen in entirety, in sequence, until the grey before sunrise entered the house and the land without began twittering. Now I go back only to the moments of desperation, when the man I was back then is at pains to clear his name.

'And you insist that you had no previous knowledge of the family, in any significant way?'

When Curtin speaks, there is compassion in his voice. It was my definite feeling at the time that he believed me. Or that he at least trusted my fundamental innocence. Nothing has changed that sense. When he speaks, he sounds as if he is trying to help me.

'In no significant respect,' I say. Initially, I seem determined to respond to them in their own terms. 'No.'

'Meaning?'

The younger one says this, from the margins. He sounds farther from the mic. His voice is sharper, couched in echoes, like a nail rattling around inside a tin can. It has a sniping quality to it. He never speaks complete sentences. He fires words, fragments, whenever he thinks he has me.

'Meaning,' I say, with some mild amusement, 'I had no knowledge of the family.'

'Not what the librarian says.'

I say nothing and my reticence, I concede, sounds uncomfortable. I remember feeling acute embarrassment then. I doubt how much they know. Until they tell me, I'm pretending to have no idea what they mean. Curtin resumes where his junior colleague has left me dangling.

'It seems the librarian in the town has come forward with details of your *research*.' There is an infinitesimal pause there, before that final word is pronounced so particularly. The pronunciation is clearly a matter of delicacy, nothing meaner, and yet the younger one can be heard to guffaw in the background. 'What might you like to tell us about that?'

I can be heard to snuffle at this point. I had forgotten going to the reference section of the library. I honestly thought nothing of it.

'I did have some curiosity about the family,' I say, 'especially after the first sister disappeared.'

'Curiosity?'

'Fascination. It was quite a story, you have to admit. But I assume everyone had the same fascination, didn't they? I don't believe I was alone in my fascination.'

'Really?'

'By the sounds of it, from what the girl told me, Hazel

Slattery's fascination was far greater than mine. You'd do well to speak with her.'

'Take it as read that we will speak to whomsoever we need to speak to.' Curtin sips from his tea mug here. 'Was there any particular reason for your own curiosity?'

Did he have a pipe? Or have I just dreamed that detail for the purposes of verisimilitude? Once, doubtless, he would have stoked up in that room. Those days were long gone, even back then. Instead he flaked plug with a little stainless-steel knife and rolled the flakes between his palms. The pipe sat dry and cold on the table between us. Occasionally Curtin held it to his lips and tapped its rim with a matchbox as if creating suction. If you wear headphones and crank up the volume, you can almost hear something of that, the dry suck down the chamber of the pipe, the matches tumbling in their box.

'I knew Harry and Sheila,' I can be heard to say. 'Knew? I still know Sheila, obviously. And I said the funeral mass for poor Harry. Sheila and Harry were their only neighbours in the close?' There is a minor rising terminal here. I am not sure, clearly, if they understand who I mean. In the absence of any grunt of assent, I carry on. 'Sheila kept on at me about calling up, particularly after the young mother disappeared. I was reluctant. They'd never been to mass, and I didn't really trust my ability to comfort them. Also, to be frank, they seemed in a world of their own up there, and a fairly peculiar world at that.'

'So you decided to find out more for yourself?'

'I did.' I laugh at this point. Why do I laugh? Embarrassment again? Perhaps a bit of that. I think I saw then, for the first time, how pathetic I must have looked across the table, red-faced and sweating, reluctantly admitting to chasing details of one young woman who had vanished. 'She just kept nagging, Sheila did, about the girls up the close and the weird life they had. So, yes, I did go up to the reference section to read back issues of the local paper, if that's what you mean by *research*. Is that so terrible? And, like I say, it doesn't sound like I was the only one. And I didn't make any bones about it. There was no cloak-and-dagger, as it were. I asked and waited at the table and had the papers brought to me.' I laugh again. I dearly wish that I didn't laugh in those gaps, but I do and it just sounds bad. 'In broad daylight.'

'We know all that,' Curtin says. 'You're only admitting to something we told you.' He laughs as well, but gently. 'But that's not the question, is it?' There is a quiet insistence in everything he says, one that I admire. I think, if I recall correctly, that I admired his quiet insistence even then. 'The question is, why? Why, apart from perfectly natural curiosity, did you go out of your way to read up about that particular family?'

They know, I remember thinking. They know that I called up, that I watched the sister and the daughter sunbathing. They are telling me that they know. They are giving me a chance to admit to it before they admit to knowing. They are testing my credibility.

'Because, I suppose, I knew that I was going to have to call up to the house, reluctantly, and because I wanted to know for myself what I was calling up to.'

'And so you did?' Curtin asks.

'Did what?'

'Call up.'

There is no discernible question mark at the end of that. However often I flick back and replay that phrase, it still sounds more statement than enquiry. They know.

'I did,' I say eventually. 'Indeed I did.'

'Go on.'

Someone saw. I was seen calling at their door. I was seen slipping down their rear access and peering through one of the wooden partition fences that divide the gardens. Whoever it was saw me came forward after the story broke.

'I called up one midweek afternoon. I rang the front doorbell. There was no answer. I was about to turn and go home. But I could hear life around the back, so I went down the lane between number five and number six, which also takes you through to the back of number seven. Just to say hello.'

'And did you?'

'Did I what?'

'Say hello . . .'

'Not exactly.'

'Go on.'

'I saw the sister and the child through the fence, in their garden.'

'The sister?'

'The girl's auntie, her mother's twin, lived with them. I thought you had spoken with her first time round. Martina.'

'*Martina.*' Curtin says that like one impressed by the depth of research, but possibly mocking with it. 'Good man.'

I wish I could erase my uttering of her name. I wish I could delete the illusion of intimacy my saying of her name creates. I say, 'Or at least I assume that's who it was.'

'But you didn't make yourself known to them?'

'I didn't, I couldn't. They were sunbathing – nothing on almost.'

'More than we bargained for,' the younger one yelps. He claps, too, and you can hear Curtin shushing him. They had no idea about any of this. They had just been fishing, sifting debris.

'So you rang the bell, you say.' Curtin is recapping slowly. 'Nobody answered. Then you went around the back because you could hear life.'

'Correct.'

'And you watched the two girls, topless as the man says, through the fence. For how long was this?'

'No time at all.'

'If you had to put a number on it? In minutes . . .'

'Couple of minutes at the very most.'

He looked amazed, Curtin did. When I said a couple of minutes, his eyes widened like I had said a couple of hours. He wrote in a notebook, with a stainless-steel pen. Or, rather, he held the pose before writing, nib inches above the paper.

'I understand it doesn't look great,' I say. 'But it happened only once, and it was a complete accident.'

'An accident?' When the younger one asks that, he is being sarcastic in a way that throws me. 'You still had a good peep for yourself?'

'I don't think that's altogether fair.' It is around this point that my voice starts to sound animated. Alongside Curtin's measured tones, it becomes excited even. 'Look, I went around to make myself known, okay? Once I saw the state they were in, I could hardly say hello, could I?' A further gap in which, I remember, they just stared blankly back. I can barely listen to myself. 'It was an awkward situation that I left as quickly as I could. And, by the way, there was no row between Martina and the father. The girl told me she just vanished too.'

'She told you that?'

'She did.'

I don't call them fools, but I remember wanting to while Curtin and his sidekick leaned into one another and conferred. They had been trawling for Martina, but until that moment it had never occurred to them to ask me if the girl had said anything of her auntie's whereabouts.

'And the reason you were at their house in the first place?' It is Curtin who asks this, with an air of finality. At first, I say nothing in response to this question. I have, my refusal says, gone over this clearly and honestly already. This lasts until Curtin prompts: 'Remind us.'

'Their neighbour Sheila kept begging me to call and see them,' I repeat, with a sliver of childish petulance. 'By all means ask her if you don't believe me. That kind of thing is my job, much as this kind of thing is yours, I imagine.'

'Was.' He was, I remember, grinning at me.

'What do you mean?'

The younger one is grinning cruelly at me when he says, '*Was* your job.'

I was not held in custody as such, nor was I charged with anything. I was, however, moved immediately to a parochial residence in another town nearby while my house was subject to the scrutiny of the force. That was a period, lasting months, which felt like unofficial house arrest. There seemed to be a squad car parked permanently out on the road, and no end of peers nearby to invigilate me. My movements were certainly not my own.

I was surrounded by three clean-shaven, ruddy-cheeked lads immersed in their various community schemes. To them, I was an ageing warhorse fallen on hard times. I went months there, feeling like a sibling returned from the equator in some minor disgrace. My presence was completely passive: speaking only when spoken to, and spoken to only collectively to be made to feel included; sitting hours in some seldom-used reception room, listening to the world's murmur elsewhere; being looked in on, if only to check that I was still there, and asked if there was anything I needed.

'Anything you need,' my new young colleagues pleaded, 'just let us know and we'll fetch it for you.'

'You're very good.'

'Anything at all.'

'My car?'

Anything but my car, it seemed. My car had already been classified as evidence, of what heaven only knows, and was out of commission. Besides, a car meant freedom of a kind that must have been no longer available to me. They glanced at one another and managed to become distracted by something completely unrelated: a microwave pinging in the background, or schoolgirls yelping out on the pavement. They swapped places, as if by rota, making certain that I was alone as little as possible.

'Anything at all,' they bleated, once the car had been removed from the options menu.

'Thank you.'

They were nice lads, to be fair, fresh-faced curates and novices far younger than myself. They behaved much as I would have done at their age. It must have been strange for them to have the likes of me in their midst. They wanted to seem as natural as they could manage. But the truth is I was news, and that fact created an invisible exclusion zone around me, one they were too timid to consider breaching. Instead, they went about their daily routines and took turns invigilating me from a safe distance. They feigned indifference to my presence and, I suspect, whispered excitedly about me out of earshot. For the first time in any of their lives, they were close to the centre of something that felt significant. They found themselves on the inside, and people hung on their every titbit. Otherwise, they worked hard at concealing that excitement from me. They popped their heads around the door, as if they had forgotten I was there, asked what I was watching on the telly, then retreated.

I remember that sitting room too well. The peat-brown three-piece suite, the mantelpiece empty of any ornaments, the electric fire with crystals illuminated by a flickering light, the placeless landscapes on opposing walls, the patterns on the wallpaper and carpet bleeding into one another . . . I will never forget it. It was a place devoid of love. Nobody cared enough to fill those empty spaces with things. What things were sprinkled about were sparse and there only as a matter of routine. Whoever had chosen those things had done so decades before and with a carelessness that remained almost palpable. The room was not loved by its inhabitants, the room seemed to say, nor were its inhabitants themselves loved.

Every once in a blue moon, I was collected and driven there. Where? No one place, but rather several different places and at irregular intervals. Specifically? I am no longer sure. I remember those autumnal months like one whose movements were involuntary and blindfolded. It was a market town initially, a wide street with a statue on an island in drizzle. When we pulled in to a standstill, people crowded around the vehicle and shouted. Some carried cameras. I was advised to cover my head with a stone-coloured mac, belonging to no one, which was lying on the back seat. It was, the driver said, for my own good. Apart from Curtin's, the names escaped me: I was told them once, on my initial arrival, but was too dazed to take them in. Thereafter, it was assumed that I knew. They stood and shook my hand every time. They even thanked me for joining them, as if I'd had a choice.

I waited for them to bring up the fact that I did tell my cleaner it would be fine to leave me alone with the girl, having led the authorities to believe that she would stop the night with us. I assumed that this had come up in the course of their interviews with her. I wondered if they were knowingly withholding this, waiting to see whether or not I would volunteer the information. I got it into my head that it was a test of my innocence. They were waiting for me to be the one to leap, as they had done with the sunbathing incident. A couple of times I nearly did. I wondered if volunteering yet more truth, however suspect it made me look, would win their trust. But I could never piece the right words together in my head. Over several weeks, it became clear to me that they had no clue. So I sang dumb.

Every such outing ended with me being ferried back in time for the evening meal. The lads did their own cooking and cleaning, of which they were terribly proud. My presence at the dinner table at first rendered them tongue-tied.

They didn't know what to say, neither to me nor to one another with a suspect in their midst, and confined themselves to the smallest talk conceivable. I tried to engage them in chat about football. They knew nothing. I tried even to ask them about Curtin, if any of them had ever crossed his path. I thought I might as well use their curiosity about me to satisfy my own. Nothing again. Gradually, however, they came back with scraps. They had asked others, in passing, and brought little facts to me. I knew they would. It was too good to resist, trafficking trivia ostensibly on my behalf. As that damp winter took hold, and I became more of a fixture and the story gathered dust, they rediscovered their tongues enough to chat across me. Inevitably, I graduated into their little running joke.

'And how was your day?' one would ask, while the others tried not to splutter.

'The same,' I would say.

'No little jaunt to town?'

'No jaunt to town.' I would feel myself blushing. I'd never felt so ancient or beyond the pale. 'Not today.'

Nights were spent together, gazing at a screen in that front room. Once, out of nowhere, midway through the evening news, my own ageing face flickered across and the voiceover reported my name. Then the grey mac in which I was partially shrouded slipped under escort into an open entrance. A couple of seconds, tops. The lads froze. Even the world without seemed to freeze. I should have said something, made light of it.

'Yes.' One of them coughed, rising hastily to insert a disc. 'Indeed.'

After that, our evening's viewing was confined to films. I

had no choice in what was shown. The choice went in a rota that never stopped at me. Once the set-up was complete, the ceiling lights were lowered and I sat back closest to the door while all manner of flesh writhed before us. I had heard that such viewing had become commonplace among the younger generation, but it was foreign to me. Instead of watching it, I watched them watching it. What a tragic path we have chosen, I thought. They will probably never know such carnal abandon, such 'passion', for want of a better word. They will desire it and never get near it. It was like watching bullocks penned in the same field for far too long. The nearest they would ever get to it was that gloomy space. I remember their competing colognes, and the shine off their high foreheads and gelled hair. I remember their silence.

Mostly, after a fashion, I closed my eyes. I blanked out the groans and whimpers. Over time, I learned to recognize the moment when I could slip away upstairs unnoticed.

About twice a month my door was tapped on last thing at night. 'Up and ready early,' one of the lads would bellow in. I assumed they had been told to warn me, though I could never understand why it seemed preferable to the authorities to tip off my junior colleagues rather than simply tell me.

'Okay,' I would call back. 'Thank you.'

Those nights were not great for sleep. I would lie there listening to rain on the slates, would rise in blackness before any alarm or call or daylight, shave, shower and wait unbreakfasted in the front room downstairs.

For what? Interviews, several interviews, in a series of different stations. They were, I quipped, my stations of the cross. Curtin and his crew kept insisting that I avail myself of legal representation. So certain was I of my own innocence that, every time they insisted, I thumbed heavenwards and said I already had the only representation I needed.

Listening to the interviews now, they become inter-changeable. I describe everything that happened from the moment that my front door started banging: the wild crea-ture on my step; the first night and the law's presence among us; the Sunday and my visit back to that house with the girl; everything she told me by my fire while the rain fell in tor-rents without; what she asked of me on the landing and how I responded; what I heard in the darkness and will never forget.

'I did contact the local station,' I say once. 'Late the second afternoon.'

'You called and spoke with someone?'

'I did. I called around half past five, to say I was taking her over to the house to fetch her computer, in case any of you landed and wondered where we were.'

'No,' Curtin says. 'No record of that.'

'Somebody must have.'

Thereafter, their number rang out and my line went dead. The world seemed to recede the harder I tried to reach it.

'What happened that nobody came or answered?'

'You don't know?' Curtin asks.

'I wouldn't ask if I knew.'

'The courthouse went up.'

'What does *went up* mean?'

'As in *in smoke*. It went up, and it went on hours.'

'I thought I saw something all right,' I say. 'I honestly didn't know that. But that doesn't make her stopping with me a second night, alone, my choice or doing.'

'Nobody is suggesting that it does.'

'I was left to my own devices, such that they were, and placed in an impossible position.'

The less they contribute, the more I babble. Doubtless this is part of the technique. I was left alone and did what best I could. With each fresh insistence, my pitch increases, my animation grows. Even now and here, many years later, I seem intent on digging myself into a deeper hole. I sound ever more guilty.

My brother came. Nobody told me he was coming. We hadn't seen one another in the flesh for a couple of decades by then, not since our mother's funeral. I had given his details, months before, when the authorities asked if they could contact someone on my behalf, but had forgotten. I drifted off one of those afternoons in the front room, and when I came to a heavy-set man was sitting next to me on the sofa. He was smiling. He said, 'How you doing?' and patted my knee. He looked familiar, but I couldn't for the life of me put a name to his face. Then it clicked.

'Are you really here?'

'I sure am,' he said. He was laughing. 'I'm really here.'

Even then I wondered if I was still asleep and his presence was just in my head. I had difficulty crediting it. Was he stopping on the way to somewhere else, or had he come just to see me? I had been so long alone by then. His familiar face seemed initially an apparition, a piece of wishful thinking, a daydream that had to be little more than a by-product of exile and solitude.

'Hey,' he said. He said it softly. He patted my knee again. 'Come on.'

Until he said that, I hadn't realized I was blubbing. I could feel my throat catch and tears welling hot in the corners of my eyes. One of the young lads, whichever of them was on duty, made to enter the room, but he had scarcely got his head around the door when my brother said, 'Thank you,' coldly and the door dragged shut again. He had, I presume, met the lads. They would have let him in. He had already formed, I could tell, an unflattering opinion of them. He even shook his head, my brother did, and I laughed, too, and struggled upright in my seat.

'You're pretty beat up.'

'I'm grand,' I said, blowing my nose and clearing my throat at once. 'What's with the accent and the freckles?'

We smiled, both of us.

'You're *grand*,' he said, in such a way as to imply that he hadn't said that word in years and had forgotten what it meant. He peered around the decor, lamp-lit in winter gloaming. 'Sure you are.'

He stayed a week. He stayed in the only four-star hotel in the area, a dozen miles out the main road away from town. He made calls on my behalf, sought advice, talked to people. He set up another 'meeting', at which he would be present and would be prepared to force the issue. He played golf in the mornings, on the course attached to the hotel. He hired a 'rental', as he called it, and brought me on spins most afternoons. Once I asked him if my leaving the house was allowed. He said something dismissive about them trying to stop me. We had grown up at the far end of the country, so there were no old haunts to revisit. It was just a question of fresh air. The week he was there, around the middle of December, was clear and freezing. He liked, I remember, high points. He liked small roads that climbed hills to a view that took in a dome of deepening blue on all sides. We would park in the gate to some field and stand out and exhale white clouds.

'You can tell me what you saw,' he said, out on one of those spins. 'Really.'

'I saw nothing,' I told him. '*Really.*' I think he blushed then, or maybe it was just the cold. I was marking his card for him. He meant that if I cared to tell him the truth I had been withholding, it would be safe with him. 'But nobody will listen to that. They all want me to be guilty.'

'Do you believe that?'

'Do I believe that? I do. I really do.'

'All anybody wants,' he said, 'is for you to be honest.'

'I'm being honest. Do you not think I'm being honest?'

'Sure I do.'

'No, you don't,' I said. 'You don't believe me and you don't really understand.'

'Tell me.'

'It's the bloody collar, isn't it? It corners you into a story in which all fingers point your way. Nobody wants me to be honest. They just want me to admit to doing and seeing things that I neither did nor saw.' When he said nothing, I said, 'And do you know what?'

'What?'

'Sometimes I'm tempted to do just that. Sometimes I'm tempted to admit to a guilt that is not mine, if only to feel the warmth of your and everyone else's forgiveness.'

'Don't.' He wrapped one hand around the back of my neck, my little brother did, and pulled me towards him. 'Don't even dream about it.'

He cut an impressive figure. I was proud of him, and yet the prouder of him I felt, the stranger he seemed. To me he had always remained the ragamuffin who vanished on the eve of his first holy communion and appeared in half-light in our yard with a stray goat and howled blue murder in the bath after being told he couldn't keep it. Now here he was, grey hair and frameless specs, managing the world with a quiet brusqueness. The other side of him, the gentleness, seemed reserved exclusively for me. I felt singled out for it; for his kindness, that is. Certainly the lads treated me differently. Their little digs stopped. Whenever he was present, waiting for me in the kitchen, say, they hovered around and made small talk in their best voices. When he dropped me off, and drove away without coming in or even getting out of the car, I would look in to bid them goodnight and they would pause their film and ask me where we had driven for our spin.

'We have a saying. Perhaps you're familiar with it. "Shit or get off the pot"?'

I have replayed this moment countless times. The grooves in the disc, if grooves there are, must be wearing thin. It sounds harsh, transcribed baldly like that, but it was not said harshly. It is my brother who says it. This is on the final disc, and is the longest unbroken segment. He had this enviable way of coming to the point without raising his pitch or playing tough. He was smiling, mildly, when he said it. At Curtin, whom he seemed to like, and the understudy seated in the fringes of the light. You can even hear Curtin chuckle. He knew immediately what was being said.

'Not in so many words,' Curtin says, obviously amused.

We can be heard to chuckle here as well. 'But the point is well made.'

This was the issue my brother kept returning to, when he and I spoke alone at dinner in the evenings in his hotel, how they seemed to want the period of suspicion to drift indefinitely. That was why he had flown over the Atlantic, the primary reason, at his own expense. In the initial fog, I had offered them his name. Unbeknown to me, he had spoken several times with Curtin over the phone, but there is only so much you can insist upon from the far side of the ocean. He flew in, a fortnight before Christmas, to demand on my behalf a resolution either way. When he first told me that this was what he intended to demand, I joked that I wanted a resolution only if it went in my favour; otherwise it could drift as indefinitely as they cared to let it. My brother just continued to scribble notes.

'Can you tell us what the girl said about Martina?' Curtin says.

'Only that she disappeared as well.'

'You know this for a fact?'

'I know only what the girl told me. She told me that her auntie went out one night, the way she always did, and never returned.'

'As far as we're aware, this was never reported.'

'The girl told me that her father said to say nothing to anyone. For fear that it would look bad, apparently.'

'Look,' my brother says abruptly. He says it to Curtin. He wants to return to his original point. He wants to draw a line under their questioning of me. 'As I see it, you've got nothing. We are requesting, respectfully, that you acknowledge this and give my brother back his life.'

'Blood not good enough for you?'

It is the younger one who says this. The more I listen to the discs, the more it's clear that this is his role. Curtin never says any of this stuff. He leaves all this to his pitbull and gets to play the avuncular inquisitor, the way it happens on the shows.

'Excuse me?' My brother didn't much care for the younger one. He told me so. You can hear the irritation. 'Really?'

'It's true,' Curtin says. He inserts a long space. He used his pipe for punctuation, as some people might begin a tale and fill their mouths with food and leave you hanging. 'We found a patch of blood.' They must have known this for months. They had been biding their time. 'We found blood on the sheet in your spare room.'

'I know nothing about that,' I say. I was looking at my brother when I say this.

'We know nothing of this,' he tells them, as if they haven't heard me. 'And you're certain the blood is the girl's?'

'We can't know that,' Curtin says. 'We have nothing to test it against.'

'Which is presumably why you haven't raised it before now.'

'Correct.'

Curtin, I remember, glanced sideways when he replied. The younger one wasn't, I decided, supposed to have said that. He had said it only out of frustration. Curtin was smoothing over the impact, the cracks.

'It was hers.' My voice says this, though it scarcely sounds as if I realize I'm saying it. I sound like one realizing something only as they speak. 'The blood. It was hers.' I was thrown at first. Then I recalled the phrase my cleaner had used and parroted it unthinkingly. 'In her flowers.'

'Excuse me?' Curtin asks.

They all laugh. Even the uniform in shadow over towards the door does. Even my own brother.

'She was in her flowers,' I say, composing myself. 'It's how my cleaner termed that time of the month.' I remember how I had to keep reminding myself, inside, that this was the truth, however much it sounded otherwise.

'Are you telling us she had her period when she stayed with you?'

'Yes,' I say, 'that's exactly what I'm telling you. My cleaner escorted the girl up to her room, and when she came back down she told me that she was in her flowers.' My brother was staring sideways at me. He wanted me, I think, to stop speaking. 'The very phrase she used. I asked her what it meant. I asked her what that phrase meant and she said "time of the month".'

'Hence the blood,' Curtin says.

'When you say you have nothing to test it against . . .' My brother's accent is smooth and curved at the edges. 'What does that mean?'

'It means we have no samples, fingerprints or DNA, that we know to be definitively hers.' The lads had told me that Curtin had lost a teenage son in a car accident. Many moons before. His wife had been largely bedridden ever since, and suffered with her nerves. 'We have fingerprints from the two houses that match, all right, but who they belong to we can't be sure.' Each time I sat opposite Curtin, his boy's death hovered over his head. 'We have no certificate of birth. Apart from what must have been the father's, the vast majority of samples taken from their house have proven identical to that patch of blood. It means that we're entertaining the possibility that there might never have been any *girl*.'

Curtin drags out that last word. He intends it to sound like a gurgle. He means that 'the girl' is my phrase. He means that 'the girl' is possibly my invention.

'This is such nonsense,' I say. 'So who was it stayed in my spare room?' My pitch is raised. 'One of the sisters? Is that what you're saying?' My brother can be heard attempting to placate me in the background. 'This is cobblers!' I am actually shouting now. 'She was just a child. You spoke to her yourself, more than once. You even held her hand, remember?' I am working hard to keep my voice from breaking. 'Do you not think you might have noticed? Do you not think *I* might have noticed? She stopped two nights in my house, thanks to you shower. She sat on my knee, for crying out loud.'

Beyond this point, I cannot bring myself to listen.

One day, not long after, all of it just stopped: the questioning, the vigil, the speculation, the coverage, the disgrace . . . My cleaner had cleaned everything, including the glass from which the girl had sipped brandy and even the orange Virginia sweatshirt in which she had warmed herself. To my surprise, I found the latter folded in the airing cupboard.

Nobody came near me. Nobody called. All sacramental duties were detailed to someone else for the foreseeable future. I became a bit of a recluse. I didn't dare show my face up the street. Closed doors scared me: apart from front and back, every one of them had to be open at all times, for fear of unfamiliar sounds. I could stand in one place, as if in a trance, resurface into consciousness, forgetting what simple act it was I had commissioned of myself, and find that hours had passed. Whole evenings got lost at the foot of the stairs, waiting for a solitary creak to repeat.

I slept in the spare bed. The linen was new: you could tell by the wrapping's creases. I lay awake in the same dark she had lain in, my own face just beneath the fold of the sheets, certain at times that I could hear her footfalls amid the echoes of New Year's revellers on the road.

I even had a bath, something I hadn't done since I was a child. That was the one space they had missed. When I climbed in, there was a ring of blue all around the lower rim. It was from the words in marker that the girl had washed off her skin, a pale, diluted blue, but still intact. She must have washed in an inch of water, and all the words had blurred into a ring of scum that nobody had thought to clean. It wasn't visible from anywhere else in the room. It was only if you climbed in that it became apparent. I remember running my thumb through it, moist from the warm water, and sucking my thumb as an infant would and convincing myself that something of her was mingled in the dirty soap I was swallowing.

I was, I admit, a stranger to myself. It was as if I was retracing her steps, half expecting that, if I kept navigating backwards in her slipstream, she might come into view.

I mustered the courage to go back to the reference section. The librarian turned puce when I came in. I sat at the same table, and when she brought me the local papers in hard binding, her hand was shaking.

No trace was found of the four members of the family. For all Curtin's speculation that there may never have been a girl, I still insist on saying *four* . . . Flood, by all accounts, served time for fraud. Slattery and his wife, eccentrics though they were and doubtless still are, had been in and out of the country for much of that strange summer. Slattery has written and self-published his own version of events, in which he describes himself as being intimate with the family.

Marcus was questioned in Reading and had the word of his employers as alibi. Apparently, text messages from him had been found on the sister's phone, and vice versa. During the course of his questioning, flummoxed probably and grabbing at anything he might use in self-defence, he said some unkind things about Martina. All of it, the texts and his testimony and the emails with the woman abroad, got leaked somehow and revealed details that even I, admittedly, have used here. Poor bereaved Sheila had two separate visits from chaps in plain clothes, and agreed that it was her who had told me to visit. The courthouse did indeed go up. Suspected arson, the reports said, but that, too, proved inconclusive. I walked among its ruins some time that winter. I probably shouldn't have. Doubtless I was seen. But what harm? It was just the once, my hands full of shopping, and there was nothing much on view other than slates caved in and charred timbers.

'I have nothing more to say,' I said. I said it to Curtin. He was seated in my kitchen one of those evenings I got home. I continued unpacking my things. We had said everything that needed saying. I was in no mood to trawl back through it, to answer yet more questions. 'I have nothing more, sir, to say to you.'

'It's something else,' he said. 'I'm just its messenger.'

'Are you asking me not to shoot you?'

He spoke to me about this place. He described the arrangement as best he could. It was my brother's idea. My brother had spoken to my superiors, who had given their blessing. My brother had asked Curtin to put it to me. Curtin described what little he knew of this place, its particular nature and this family. He even seemed enthusiastic, which would be hard to countenance for anyone who knew the man. Did he phone in advance? Did he press my bell and did I answer? I don't remember any of that. All I remember is him seated at the table in my kitchen, gloves in hand, refusing anything to drink and keeping on his long grey greatcoat for the duration of what he repeatedly called 'our chat'. The place would be, he said, part appointment and part retreat.

'What does that mean?'

'You'll see.' He rose and came over to where I was leaning against the sink. For a second, I felt sure that he planned to embrace me. I felt sure, indeed, that he was planning to plant a kiss, Judas-like, on my cheek. 'Will you hear my confession?'

Without waiting for me to respond, positively or otherwise, he produced a set of wooden rosary beads, hunkered painfully onto one knee, made the sign of the cross and began to speak: 'Bless me, Father, for I have sinned . . .' I felt so grateful to him. Not since the girl on my landing had anyone addressed me as such. It was as if he was doing it intentionally, restoring a confiscated identity to me. I remember the streak of yellow that years of pipe smoke had bleached in his hair. I remember the antique brown beads pressed to his lips.

They say that when you lose a child, the pain only dulls with distance, but really never ends or goes away. They say the world greys out. Existence becomes mere muscle memory, force of habit devoid of any texture or flavour. I could not have known that Curtin would be dead before the following summer was out, that he was withering within even then, as he knelt muttering his sins at my feet. Wild horses will never drag out of me what he confessed. All I can say is that what he did confess has no direct bearing on this story.

For a time, I would continue to hear scraps by letter from my former cleaner, or an email from one of my young successors, seeking advice and letting certain facts slip. Eventually, those too dried up. Last I heard, the county had bulldozed the close and turned it into a playground where no one ever plays.

The family inhabited, it appears, a world that came apart at the seams and disappeared piecemeal. The girl's mother had worked occasionally for a couple in broadcasting. The mother's sister did a line, briefly, with the lad on night security on the site. After he had upped sticks, she kept donning her finery and going up by herself to his empty caravan. Her sombrero was indeed found hanging on a wall in one of Flood's townhouses. The father, jobless, ignored rent payments and warnings that the bank was taking back Flood's land. There were never any Poles, except for those in Paul's head. The cessation of amenities – water, electricity – only accentuated whatever concluding fantasy he and the girl shared.

All of which is clear enough. Up to this point, the story

can be mapped and followed with some certainty. From there, however, its path tapers into long grass. Reason, with all its explanations, takes us this far and no farther.

'Write down what you saw,' my brother said, the last time we spoke on the phone. It was November then, the one just gone or perhaps the one before that, a blaze of olive logs in the range.

'I saw nothing.' I was plenty angry with him. 'I told you. I told you and everyone else.'

'You must have seen something,' my brother said. 'Write what you did see. Send it to me when it's finished.'

So I wrote what I did see, what I think I saw and what I know I heard. But I will not be the man they want me to be. I will not wear their scapegoat's crown of thorns. And yet the more truth I tell, the more I seem determined to write myself closer to the centre of a story that should never have been mine. In the time that has elapsed since last we spoke, I have sent my brother half a dozen versions but have heard nothing back. I try calling him. The system's recorded message asks me to recheck the number and dial again. Maybe what has happened to me, and keeps on happening, is merely something that happens to all of us with age. The world depopulates. Gradually our loved ones stop answering. Where has my brother gone? Where does everyone go?

Stick to a story long enough, and the story sticks to you. It has become like a private garden I return to in my head and in which I sit alone. Every now and then I make amendments: prune something, plant elsewhere. I have tinkered so much that I cannot be certain which flowers were here and which were introduced by me. I have assumed the girl's bare bones and seeded into them colours, textures, incidentals that she surely couldn't have shared with me at my hearth. Every time I click 'attach' and 'send', I tell myself to leave it to one side, that it is done. But some fresh thing reveals itself and the story alters. Once my brother responds, if ever he does, once he tells me that he has read my story and believes its every word, it will be taken from my hands.

Until he does, it falls to me, in paradise, to keep the chimney warm, the roof from caving in, the gypsies from plundering. What did I see? A biplane buzzes overhead. Hip-hop pulses from a post van left running, the driver's door hanging open. Someone I have never seen before is tending blossoms in the grotto.

I pray that I may forget. Or, failing that, that I may at least remember what forgetting feels like. I dream sometimes that I am retracing a track through woods to where the girl will be, but when I reach the spot there is only a hole burned in the earth where she stood. I keep thinking I see her face at some or other market, across stalls of hardware or rotting fruit. I see her as she appeared on my step, not as she might be now. An owl's shrieks above the courtyard's black are like screams in another room. Some evenings, when I am full of hope fuelled by little more than a late blast of cloudless gold, my door darkens out of nowhere and my peace is shaken asunder by banging.

Conor O'Callaghan is originally from Dundalk, and now divides his time between Dublin and the North of England. *Nothing on Earth* is his first novel.

The Hurley Maker's Son
A Memoir

Patrick Deeley

Patrick Deeley's train journey home to rural East Galway in autumn 1978 was a pilgrimage of grief: his giant of a father had been felled, the hurley-making workshop silenced.

From this moment, Patrick unfolds his childhood as a series of evocative moments, from the intricate workings of the timber workshop to the slow taking apart of an old tractor and the physical burial of a steam engine; from his mother's steady work on an old Singer sewing machine to his father's vertiginous quickstep on the roof of their house. There are many wonderful descriptions of the natural world and delightful cameos of characters and incidents from a not-so-long-ago country childhood.

In a style reminiscent of John McGahern, the beautifully paced prose captures the rhythms, struggles and rough edges of a rural life that was already dying even as he grew. This is an enchanting, beautifully written account of family, love, loss, and the unstoppable march of time.

'Suffused with warmth and joy and an ineffable sadness'
DONAL RYAN

'An elegiac glimpse of a time that's long gone'
SUNDAY EXPRESS

'Every sentence rings true, like an axe biting into seasoned wood, a hurley striking the ball cleanly'
THEO DORGAN

'A wonderfully evocative memoir'
SEAN O'ROURKE, RTÉ RADIO 1

All We Shall Know

Donal Ryan

'Martin Toppy is the son of a famous Traveller and the father of my unborn child. He's seventeen, I'm thirty-three. I was his teacher.'

Melody Shee is alone and in trouble. Her husband doesn't take her news too well. She can't tell her father yet because he's a good man and this could break him. She's trying to stay in the moment, but the future is looming – larger by the day – while the past won't let her go. What she did to Breedie Flynn all those years ago still haunts her.

It's a good thing that she meets Mary Crothery when she does. Mary is a young Traveller woman, and she knows more about Melody than she lets on. She might just save Melody's life.

'A stunning piece of work, utterly truthful
and emotionally powerful'
JOSEPH O'CONNOR

'A democratic work of genius . . . I was
entranced by it. Buckled by it'
SEBASTIAN BARRY

'To his raw, wounded and grieving characters Donal Ryan
says: If you are still breathing, you can be redeemed'
COLIN BARRETT

'Ryan's strongest work to date . . . an exquisite account of
womanhood, friendship, prejudice and tradition that is both
intimate in scale and awesome in achievement'
IRISH INDEPENDENT